FIRST BLADE

THE AWAKENING SERIES - BOOK ONE

JANE HINCHEY

ABOUT THIS BOOK

Georgia Pearce possesses remarkable psychic abilities. When she discovers an ancient dagger hidden in her workshop, she knows it can only mean one thing. Trouble.

Trouble arrives in the form of Zak Goodwin, an entity more powerful - and definitely sexier - than any she's come across before. However, when a horde of dangerous vampires show up and threaten Georgia and her sister, she has no choice but to ask Zak for help.

Along with a shifter cop, a band of vampire warriors, and her own psychic skills, Georgia sets out to stop the awakening of an immortal vampire who has the power to destroy the world — and discovers that staying alive isn't nearly as dangerous as falling in love.

If you like fast-paced paranormal romantic suspense, thrilling heroes, and sassy, kick-ass heroines then you'll love the first installment of the Awakening series by Jane Hinchey.

Buy First Blade to begin the breathtaking adventure of Georgia and Zak today!

AUTHOR'S NOTE

Hey! Welcome to the weird and wacky world of my imagination! I hope you enjoy your time here.

If you love your supernatural adventures with heat and sizzle, then you're going to enjoy the journey ahead — at least, I think you will.

Fair warning, most of my books are cozy mysteries. This is definitely not one of those books. While there is mystery, intrigue, and suspense, there is also swearing, violence and sex. If this your jam, read on. If not, one of my cozy mysteries may suit you better.

No matter your preference, I'd love to connect with you.

Sign up for my newsletter: https://JaneHinchey.com/subscribe

Join my VIP Reader Group:
www.JaneHinchey.com/LittleDevils

Ready to get started?
I'll see you on the other side!

xoxo

Jane

CHAPTER
ONE

With his hands dripping in blood and the severed head of a demon lying at his feet, Zak took no time in savoring the victory—he'd never seen demons in these numbers before. If he and his men intended to get out of this alive, they needed to stay focused. The putrid sulfur of their stench assaulted his senses, making his eyes burn.

Across the room, Aston was battling two demons, a sword in one hand, dagger in the other. Dainton was at his back, lunging at an already wounded demon; his sword slashed deeply across its torso revealing flesh and bone.

Cole, Kyan, and Heath were knee-deep in bloody corpses, ripping off heads and tossing them, wading

1

their way through the gore, eyes burning red with the thrill of the fight. He'd taught his team well, and they hadn't disappointed him.

Loud explosions could be heard from outside, rattling the building. A flash of lightning erupted from a demon's hand and snaked across the room toward him. *Fucking demons.* Zak snatched the demon by its neck. He lifted it over his shoulders, snapped its body over his knee, and then flung it aside. Frank was tangling with three other demons, wincing when one sent him smashing into a wall. Zak was there in an instant, pulling Frank to his feet, pausing with his hand on his shoulder, healing him. With a slap on the back in thanks, Frank jumped back into the fray.

Heath was throwing demons across the room, bodies flying. Zak caught another, this time tearing out its throat with his fangs before tossing the body. Another flew past, and he grabbed, twisting off its head and throwing it like a soccer ball.

Another explosion, louder than the first, rocked the building. The ground bucked, toppling Zak's team and demons alike.

Veronica appeared in the doorway, hands against the frame as she struggled to remain on her feet with the building trembling and buckling around them.

"Zak!" she shouted, "we have to get out. Now! The house is collapsing. The fuckers have rigged explosives."

"Everyone out!" Zak bellowed, eyes scanning the room for his team. Frank, his head of security, was on the far side, shoving the body of a demon off himself as he surged back to his feet. Aston, Dainton, Cole, Kyan, and Heath made up the rest of his team, and what a team of warriors they were. Elite fighting machines, they were highly skilled at what they did—and not a bad bunch of blokes in the bargain. The six of them headed toward the door, flinging demons as they went.

Parts of the ceiling started to collapse as they hurried down the hallway. The lights flickered, then went off, but none of them needed light to see. Demons still came at them, but the warriors flicked them off as if they were nothing more bothersome than a fly.

Crashing through the house's back door, they tumbled out onto the lawn. Veronica had already evacuated the domestic staff, a group of four humans who stood huddled behind her, dazed and afraid.

Zak stood on the lawn and watched as his house collapsed with a roar, the center caving in first, the roof buckling inwards like it was being sucked into a black hole. Within minutes the house was razed, nothing remaining but a plume of dust.

His warriors stood in formation around him, watching, as he did, with no emotion as their home was destroyed. While the loss of his home pissed him off, it wasn't the end of the world. He had plenty of resources; finding shelter for them was not an issue. What had his blood boiling was the fifty or more demons who were facing them from the other side of the pile of rubble that used to be his home.

Zak's control slipped, and power coursed through him. He'd forgotten what it felt like to just let go and let his magic absorb him.

Frank glanced at him; he could feel the power in the air that was now filled with electricity. He ordered the others back, away from Zak. They didn't want to be close to him when he unleashed the full potential of his power.

Zak raised his hands, the air bent around him as his power unfurled in a red haze. The demons were bounding like hellhounds across the debris, intent on getting to him and ripping him to pieces. They had no chance.

Releasing his magic, a pulse of raw energy swept from his open hands in a wide arc before him, blasting the demons into oblivion before they even got close. They disintegrated in front of him, no blood, no bones, simply piles of ash. Felled in one swoop, the air was now still and eerily silent.

"Holy Fuck!" Heath muttered behind him. "That was some red hot shit right there."

Zak turned to face his warriors, his eyes still glowing red.

"You are well?" His gaze swept across them, searching for injuries. They nodded in reassurance, a few minor scrapes, clothing torn and covered in blood, but unhurt. He pulled in several deep breaths, quieting his magic, letting it settle back inside of him. Now that it'd had a taste of the action, it wanted to come out and play. Zak had no intentions of letting that happen—his house may have been destroyed, but he'd be damned if he would allow himself to cut loose and destroy the rest of the world, for that was what would happen if he truly allowed his magic to take over.

Frank stepped up to him and murmured quietly, "Your ring." He nodded at Zak's hand.

The ring was understated in design, a pattern of three ribbons intertwined with different shades of platinum and gold that adorned the ring finger on his right hand. Only now, one of the rivers was no longer platinum but glowed red as it flowed through the design. A beautiful but chilling effect as it twisted and wove around his finger as if alive.

"It has been activated." His words were calm, belying the anxiety that suddenly rushed through him. For the ring to be activated, the dagger had not only been found, but that too had been awakened with blood. This wasn't good, wasn't good at all.

"**O**uch!" Georgia pulled her hand out of the hidden cavity she'd just found behind a stone brick in the old stable wall. She'd been moving boxes when she'd noticed one of the handmade bricks was sitting slightly farther back than the others. She'd pushed at it, and to her surprise, she'd heard a clicking and grinding noise, and the brick had slid backward, revealing a dark hidey-hole in the wall. Of course, she'd put her hand in to feel around to see if anything was hidden inside.

Snatching her hand back, she hoped that the sharp sting had not been the bite of a spider! Glancing down at her hand, she was somewhat relieved to see an inch-long cut on her index finger.

The cut oozed blood, but the edges looked clean—it hadn't been a jagged or particularly nasty cut. It would be easily treated with some antiseptic ointment and a band-aid.

Rising from her kneeling position in front of the wall, she crossed to her workbench and pulled the first aid kit toward her, efficiently dealing with the injury before grabbing a torch and heading back to the brick cavity, determined to see what was hidden there.

"What have you got hiding in here, hmm? Must be important to warrant all this trouble." Muttering to herself, she flicked the flashlight on and peered into the black space. The area had been hollowed out to the size of a shoebox, and there at the bottom was what looked like an old cloth with...was that a knife? Frowning, she reached her hand in, more carefully this time, and scooped her fingers beneath the fabric, carefully lifting it out. Laying the material on the floor, she smoothed it out, revealing the old, dull knife that now had a smear of her blood on its blade. She supposed it looked like a dagger rather than a knife. It was the length of her forearm with some sort of woven design on the handle. The blade looked dirty and dusty, but it wasn't rusted. Overall, it had a very medieval look. Her curiosity was definitely piqued as to why it had been hidden in her stable wall.

She returned to the workbench, pulled a clean rag out, and rubbed the dagger. As she wiped and polished, she noticed the design on the handle seemed to glow and change color. The design was beautiful, unlike anything she'd seen before. It appeared to be three ribbons, weaving around each other but twisting around the handle as well. One ribbon was gold, one silver, and the third looked red, only it wasn't a gem. Peering closely, Georgia tried to make out what the red material was; it appeared to glow in a very unusual way.

After polishing the blade to a gleaming silver, she held the dagger out in front of her and practiced a couple of thrusts with it. While it looked like it should have been heavy, it was relatively light in her grip. Putting the dagger aside, she turned her attention to the cloth it had been wrapped in.

It appeared to be leather, and after shaking out the dust, she could see faint markings on it. Peering closely, she couldn't make out if it was writing, symbols, or simply a pattern etched into the leather. She'd have to get some cleaning solution next time she was in town and see if she couldn't clean it up to get a good look at the design. In the meantime, she wrapped the dagger back in the cloth and took it with her into the farmhouse.

"GEORGIA, are you even listening to me!" Skye demanded. Georgia held the cell phone away from her ear—her sister's screeching was not helping her hangover one iota.

"I'm listening."

"Oh, for god's sake. Sober up. It's busy as hell; get your ass down here." Clearly annoyed, she hung up.

Struggling out of bed, Georgia made her way into the bathroom, wincing at the bright light. She pried her eyes open, catching sight of herself in the mirror. *Good grief.* Most of her hair had come loose from its braid and was now a wild beehive around her head; her tanned skin was an unhealthy ashen gray, and her green eyes had lost their usual sparkle, to be replaced with dull pain. Stunning, not.

The shower felt like heaven. The hot stream of water revived her as it rushed over her body; brain cells struggled to the surface, freed from the alcoholic blur of the previous night. As she tried to work some of the soreness out of her muscles, her mind returned to the dream. The same dream she'd had almost every night since finding that damn dagger a month ago.

Every night a man appeared from the recesses of her mind as if he was waiting for sleep to claim her. She couldn't see his features fully, yet he was the epitome of sensuality, of male magnetism and allure. They never touched, yet her skin burned as if he'd run his fingers across her flesh; her lips tingled as if a kiss as light as air had landed on them. He teased her in her dreams, and she yearned for him.

She'd wake in the morning, frustrated and no closer to discovering who was haunting her dreams. She figured her dreams were being invaded but couldn't determine how or why. Her ability was visions. She could touch a person and catch a glimpse of their future. Sometimes she could see the past from touching inanimate objects. The dreams were different from anything she'd ever seen or done before. Yet somehow, they were connected. She just needed to figure out how.

Never one to bother much with makeup, she quickly ran tinted moisturizer over her face, made a half-hearted effort at covering the shadows beneath her eyes, then braided her long dark hair, leaving it to dry in the braid hanging down her back. This morning, there was no hair dryer; the sound alone would make her brain melt thanks to her hangover. A swipe of lip gloss, and she was done.

Jeans and a white cotton blouse were the uniform of the day. Her generous breasts pulled against the fabric, straining to send the buttons flying, so she left the top two undone, allowing a generous view of cleavage. She'd discovered, quite by accident, that displaying 'the girls' in the shop helped close the sale a whole lot faster. Wives and girlfriends didn't appreciate the view, but the boyfriends and husbands did, and they were the ones being dragged around the antique stores on their precious days off. And they were the ones with the fat wallets.

Downtown Redmeadows was a sleepy strip of two-story buildings, mom-n-dad owned stores, and more antique shops than you could shake a stick at. Georgia and her younger sister Skye owned one of those antique stores. *Behind the Times* was nestled between a bookstore and a boutique fashion store, and quite conveniently, Georgia thought, across the road from a pub. The irony is that Skye lived in the small apartment above the shop, therefore within walking distance of the said pub. Yet it was Georgia, the lush of the family according to Skye, who lived twenty minutes out of town.

Fixing a coffee in her travel mug, Georgia hurried out to her fully restored 1942 candy apple red Ford Jailbar. It'd been forgotten in the old stable on the five acres of land she'd bought a few years ago, along with the derelict farmhouse she'd renovated and now lived in. The Jailbar had been the old town tow truck back in the day, and Georgia had been delighted to discover it rusting away in the stable.

She placed her travel mug in its holder and gunned the engine, sliding the back end out as she fishtailed the truck down the gravel driveway, stereo muted somewhat from its usual 'blasting' setting in consideration of her pounding head.

Georgia walked into *Behind the Times* exactly forty-five minutes after Skye had called.

"It's almost ten," Skye said, tapping her watch. She wore jeans and a red and white polka dot blouse tied at her waist. On her feet were red pumps, and her blonde curls were pulled up into a cute high ponytail with a red scarf tied around her head. Very retro, but it suited her.

"It's closer to nine-thirty," Georgia argued, stalking past the counter to the small office beyond.

Crammed to overflowing with a couple of filing cabinets, an old wooden desk that she really must get around to renovating, and a couple of chairs, there was barely room for one person, let alone two. Dropping her keys and phone onto the desk, she closed the door behind her and moved to stand behind the counter.

"Run off your feet?" she inquired in disbelief with an arch of a brow, indicating the handful of people browsing through the store.

"Took you so long to get here it's thinned out a bit now," Skye responded defensively. She studied her sister closely. "You look like hell."

"Thanks." Georgia shrugged, unconcerned.

"You didn't drive, did you?" Skye frowned.

"Last night? No. This morning? Yes. God, stop fussing, woman. I'm fine. I have a sturdier constitution than you."

"How did you get home?"

"Rhys dropped me. Mom." Georgia sniggered and moved away before Skye could grill her any further, spotting a young couple admiring one of her renovated bedroom suites. True to form, the young man could barely raise his eyes from her chest, but hey, it closed the sale. She rang them up, took their details, and promised the furniture would be delivered that week.

Georgia watched them leave with a slight grin twisting her lips. The couple didn't know it yet, but a bouncing baby girl was in their future.

Lunchtime rolled around, and Georgia was thinking of sneaking across the road to the pub when the bell over the front door chimed, and Rhys strode in, takeaway bag in his hands.

"Father my children!" she demanded, reaching up to give him a one-armed hug while snatching the bag away with the other. Rhys grinned and let her take it.

"Figured you could use this."

Rhys was her best friend. He was also a werewolf and a cop and easy on the retinas. Six feet, broad shoulders, short dark hair, and smoky gray eyes. His skin was tanned to a soft mocha, and Georgia had often wondered if his coloring was the same in wolf form.

"You know me so well," she mumbled around a mouthful of burger.

Rhys grabbed the takeout bag off Georgia and rummaged inside, handing a burger to Skye, then got stuck into his own. It hadn't been lost on Georgia that Skye was a victim to his confident walk and easy smile. Her eyes followed him everywhere he went. She wondered if she needed to give them a nudge in the right direction. So far, neither Skye's nor Rhys's romantic future had revealed themselves to her in any vision, so she had no clue if they were meant to be together or not.

"So, have you heard?" Rhys asked after they'd finished eating.

"Heard what?"

"You know that author you like, Zak Goodwin? Well, he's just bought the old homestead up the road from you."

"Fuck off. No! Really?"

"Wow!" Skye chimed in. "For real? What on earth for?"

"Well, you heard that his place in Elen Hills got totaled, right? Seems he wants a total change of pace, and thanks to the internet, he discovered the homestead on a real-estate site and bought the place."

"Do you think he'll live here permanently?" Skye breathed, leaning forward, her hand on Rhys's arm.

"Dunno. Guess we'll find out."

"Have you seen him yet?" Skye was, of course, referring to the best-selling author who was now Georgia's neighbor. Admittedly, his house was ten miles away, so it wasn't as if she could step out onto her back porch and spy on him. Or vice versa. Georgia's farmhouse had initially been part of his land—until it all got subdivided and sold off to bail the owners out of financial trouble.

"Nope." She was in two minds about the whole thing. She was a fan of his books. His stories were dark and violent, tales of monsters, demons, and things that go bump in the night. She loved reading them because she suspected his fictional stories were based on truth. She'd known since childhood that witches, werewolves, and vampires existed. And she'd learned just as quickly to keep your mouth shut about it, or people would think you were crazy.

"You're a fan, aren't you? I've seen his books on your bookshelf." Skye continued to prod, and Georgia blew out an exasperated breath.

"Yes. I like his books. No, I do not like, not one bit, that this place has been overrun with media and fans. Christ, I can't even get a park near our shop. I had to park blocks away and walk! And the bloody girls who come in and giggle and carry on, not wanting to buy anything, they just want to know if the great Zak Goodwin has been in our store. I'm sick of it already." She groused. The Zak Goodwin phenomenon compounded her already frayed nerves—her nights were filled with frustrating dreams that she couldn't shake. She was exhausted, leaving her frustrated, grumpy, and definitely not in the mood to deal with a bunch of fan girls.

Sensing her sister's rapidly dwindling patience, Skye ordered her back to the farm.

"It's school holidays; I can get my casuals in to lend a hand." Skye waved away her concerns for leaving her sister alone to deal with the shop. "Plus, we have some empty spaces in the shop, I need you to fill 'em, and that's not going to happen if you're working in here every day."

Skye had a point. They'd sold three large pieces in the last week. Skye had already delivered several items to the workshop; they were just waiting for Georgia to weave her magic over them. Which wasn't really magic; it was sanding, and more sanding, and painting, and sanding.

"Fine," Georgia had growled, secretly relieved to be able to work at the farmhouse for a few days. She loved the seclusion of her little piece of earth, her farmhouse, and its five acres of space. Over the last four years, she'd painstakingly renovated the house, putting her carpentry skills to use and doing most of the work herself. She gladly subbed out the plumbing and electrical re-wiring, but the rest was her own blood, sweat, and tears. She loved her place; it was her haven against the world.

Pulling into her driveway with a skid of tires and a cloud of dust, she swept into the house, making a beeline for the refrigerator and an icy cold beer. Alcohol was taking the edge off her dreams. Still, the amount she needed to consume to achieve oblivion was starting to bother even her. She'd need a new liver within a year at the rate she was going.

Slumping on the old swing on the back deck, she

propped her feet up on the coffee table. She settled back, watching the way the trees swayed, the warm, gentle breeze brushing against her skin, the distant buzz of bees as they went about their business.

The dream started out like all the others. From the darkness, a shadow moved; a tendril of smoke wound its way toward her, surrounding her. Georgia pushed against the back of the swing while the dark shadow wrapped around her. While it should have suffocated her, it didn't. It felt hot. The air around her sizzled and crackled. The shadow took shape; the smoke meshed and fused to form a solid body.

She felt the weight of him against her, his mouth against her ear as he whispered "Mine," and she melted into him. Her eyes fluttered open, and she could make out dark hair and a stubbled jaw. His tall body straddled hers, his chest broad. Her hands explored him, desperate to know him. Heat drifted off him, and then his mouth covered hers, and she was lost, her eyes closing as he became her world.

The kiss deepened, grew more urgent, and her body responded. She wanted him. Wanted him on her, around her, in her.

From a distance, she heard her name.

"Georgia?"

She tumbled out of the dream and back into

reality. Her eyes fluttered open to find Rhys staring at her, a quizzical expression drawing his brows together. She felt dizzy, unable to focus after being pulled from the dream so abruptly.

"You ok?" he asked.

Snapping herself out of it, Georgia threw him a grin, "Sure. More tired than I realized if I fell asleep sitting here!" While she wanted nothing more than to dissect her latest dream, the reality of Rhys kneeling in front of her precluded any such activity.

"Wanna beer?" she offered, leaning forward, getting ready to rise.

"I'll get it." He pushed her back gently, and she let him, easing back against the swing with a sigh. She felt oddly cold without the heat from the dream.

Rhys returned, sitting in the chair at right angles to the swing.

"That must've been some dream." He commented, watching intently. She blushed.

"Er...why?"

"You looked...hot...." Her green eyes met his, and he held her gaze, his eyes sparkling with curiosity.

Oh boy. Rhys was an attractive guy. In fact, he was downright smoking hot. Georgia already knew she didn't feel for him that way. Still, the way he was looking at her, she knew she'd inadvertently gotten his interest.

"Just a dream, I can't really remember it," she said, breaking the spell by looking beyond him. The sun was now on the horizon, the sky a stunning array of oranges and pinks, twilight settling over this side of the earth. Thankfully he took the hint.

"You missed the excitement this afternoon." He told her, taking a swig of beer. She really didn't think she had; the excitement in her dream had been plenty. Out loud she said, "Oh?"

"Yeah, one of Zak Goodwin's entourage came into your store. I'm surprised Skye didn't call you."

"She's giving me some time out. I'm not sure if I'm being punished or rewarded."

"She's worried about you. You have been burning the candle at both ends a bit lately."

"Sorry that I keep dragging you into it," Georgia apologized. If it wasn't Rhys she was out drinking with, it was usually him that she called in the early hours of the morning looking for a ride home. He'd never let her down, even though she'd often dragged him out of his bed.

"Can't you tell me what's wrong?" he leaned forward, resting his arms on his knees with his beer dangling from his fingers.

"You'd think I'm crazy. Crazier than I already am."

"I don't think you're crazy, Georgia. Don't let people who don't understand or appreciate your special skills make you think you're crazy."

"I don't even know what I am. Not really."

"You're psychic." His simple explanation should have been all she needed, but for some reason, she needed more.

"That seems such a broad definition. Psychic. If I were truly psychic, why can't I predict lotto numbers?"

Rhys pulled out his phone and started tapping on the screen before reading to her.

"Psychic: a person sensitive to things beyond the natural range of perception."

"I suppose," she grumbled, not happy with the label but not knowing what else you would call her talent.

"So what, now you're having bad dreams about being psychic?" he quizzed.

"No. Someone is...haunting my dreams."

"Haunting? Like a ghost?"

"Well, I don't think it's a ghost 'cos he only shows up in my dreams. Someone is connecting with me via my dreams—only I don't know who."

"Are they hurting you? Threatening you?"

"The opposite." She hesitated. She didn't want to share the intimate nature of the dreams with him.

"Ahhhh." From the knowing look he gave her, she guessed Rhys had figured it out for himself.

"Not going there, Rhys!" she held up her hand, palm toward him to stop whatever words were about to come out of his mouth.

"So what did Zak's lackey want?" she said, deftly changing the subject.

Rhys shrugged, "All I heard was something about carving." Georgia had several hand-carved figurines on display in the window that generated a lot of interest. Partly because they were hand-carved, but mostly because they were of vampires, werewolves, and witches. Georgia had created several eight-inch-high figurines, each depicting a different supernatural being doing what they did best—a vampire baring his fangs, a werewolf caught changing, a witch spell casting. They sold like hot cakes.

Patience wasn't her strong suit. Rather than wait for Skye to call her, she pulled out her phone and dialed her sister.

"Hey! I hear on the never-wrong grapevine of

our town that Zak Goodwin's lackey was in the store this afternoon?"

Skye chuckled. "Yes, one of his employees ducked in, asking questions about the restorative work you do and the figurines. Wanted to know if you could be commissioned."

"I hope you said yes!"

"Of course! Think of the money if Zak commissioned you to carve him a unique piece!"

"So what happened? Do we have a gig?"

"Nothing after that. They thanked me for the information and left. I guess it's wait and see."

"I hate wait and see," Georgia grumbled, slinging a glance at Rhys when he chuckled next to her.

"Rhys and I are having a beer at the farm—you wanna join?"

"Can't tonight. Have plans."

"Ooooh, you gotta date?" She felt Rhys's eyes sharpen on her. Good. A little jealousy might prod things along nicely.

"Just dinner and a movie with Sophie."

"Well, you enjoy. Say hi from me." She hung up and looked at Rhys, "Skye can't make it. She's gotta date," she lied, satisfied at the frown that pulled his brows together.

CHAPTER
FOUR

"I'm on the early shift tomorrow, gotta head off." Rhys stretched and then reached out to ruffle her hair in farewell.

"Thanks for dropping by." She waved as he jumped into his car, watching until his taillights disappeared. She liked Rhys. A lot. She'd known him since school, they'd been in the same grade, and they'd become best friends. He'd spent as much time at her house as his own. Which was why he'd joined the police force. To be like her dad, Detective Pearce. Only her dad was now dead, killed along with her mom in a car accident five years ago. Seeing Rhys always reminded her of her loss, and she cursed herself that she hadn't seen it coming. What use was a psychic gift if you couldn't save your own parents?

"Food. I need food." Two beers on an empty stomach had given her a buzz, and considering she was trying to be nicer to her liver, food seemed the appropriate, the adult and responsible, thing to do.

Rustling up some scrambled eggs, she wolfed them down while standing in the kitchen, leaning against the cupboards. She'd been eyeing the fridge, trying to decide if another beer was a smart idea, when the sound of tires crunching on gravel reached her ears. She straightened and placed her dirty plate in the sink before moving across the room to peer out the lounge room window. Her driveway was two hundred meters long, so she knew it had to be on her property if she heard a car.

A bright yellow jeep pulled up, and a tall woman stepped out. She was stunning; blonde curls danced around her shoulders and positively sparkled in the moonlight.

"Hey." Georgia opened the front door and flicked on the porch light.

"Oh. Hello." The woman slammed the jeep door closed and moved toward her. She wore a fresh, floral wraparound dress that positively shouted summertime, and on her feet were a pair of wedges that gave her added height she most definitely didn't need. The woman was several inches taller than Georgia—she wouldn't have been surprised if she was a model. She *was* surprised to sense she was a vampire. Georgia could pretty much identify a species once they were within fifty feet of her. What she also knew was that supernaturals were a lot like humans—you got your good ones, you got your bad ones.

"I'm looking for Georgia Pearce." Her voice had an unmistakable accent. One of the famous author's entourage, no doubt. She wondered if he knew he had a vampire in his midst, then kicked herself mentally. Of course, he did—*you've read his books Georgia*, she scolded herself.

"I'm Georgia." She smiled in greeting but didn't offer her hand to shake.

"My name's Veronica. I live with Zak Goodwin— we've just moved into the house up the road from you."

Georgia had seen a few photos of the woman accompanying Zak around town on the local newspaper website.

"How are you settling in?" Georgia inquired politely, feeling frumpy, overweight, and downright unattractive in front of the beautiful woman.

"A lot of work has to be done to the house, but we have a couple of rooms that are habitable while renovations are carried out. Which brings me to why I'm here. Your work has come to Zak's attention, and he would like to meet with you to discuss a couple of pieces he would like you to work on at the house."

"Oh?" Georgia raised a brow. She guessed when you were as rich as Zak, you didn't have to do all the running around yourself and could send your girlfriend on errands for you.

"Zak will explain what is required. Is seven tomorrow evening suitable? It'll give you plenty of time to freshen up," the woman eyed Georgia up and down, her distaste at Georgia's appearance evident. Georgia bristled, tempted to tell her that seven o'clock didn't suit, just to be difficult. But the truth was they needed the money a job like this would bring in. While the business was doing okay, and the rush thanks to Zak's fan girls had certainly helped, it was always a struggle to meet their financial commitments from month to month. Georgia drew enough of a wage to cover her mortgage and general living expenses but never had any left over for luxuries.

"Seven is fine. I'll see you then."

"Good." Without another word, Veronica spun on her heel and walked away.

Georgia watched until the jeep was out of sight.

Well, she thought, dusting her hands off on the pants of her jeans, this should be interesting.

Pulling out her phone, she texted Skye:

"*Just met supermodel bitch. Lives with Zak. He wants 2 meet 2 discuss job.*"

"*Fuck—he has a girlfriend?*"

"*Apparently. Veronica. Blonde bombshell—find her on Facebook.*"

"*What job?*"

"*Don't know. Going 2 visit 2moro at 7. Will call u after.*"

The following morning, after another dream-filled night of phantom touches that teased but didn't follow through, Georgia was thankful she didn't have to deal with anyone at the shop and could hole up in her workshop instead.

Her workshop was, in fact, the old stone stable behind the house; she'd gutted it and turned it into a massive workspace, with a small home gym tucked away at one end. She'd done her best to retain the character of the building. She'd replaced the rotten floorboards, had the place wired for electricity, and replaced the warped wooden windows with large shutter-style windows that she could open when the weather was nice and let the breeze flow through. Even after the renovations, she swore she could still smell horses in the old building—and loved it.

Her work gear consisted of worn denim shorts, a black tank top with washed-in paint stains, and scuffed work boots. Even in the heat of summer, Georgia wore her boots while working. Better to have hot feet than risk losing a toe if she dropped a chisel or power tool.

Georgia had always been what her mom called a *tomboy*, more comfortable in jeans and t-shirts than dresses and heels. She usually only bothered with makeup on special occasions, which were few and far between. Her one feminine wile was her hair. Georgia loved her waist-length, chocolate-colored hair with its streak of pink. Left lose it flowed in natural waves down her back, different shades of brown and gold weaving through the silken strands and peeking through from underneath were glimpses of pink. She usually wore it up in a high ponytail or a braid. While she acknowledged it would be easier to look after if she cut it shorter, she couldn't bring herself to do it.

Today she braided it in a single plait down her back. Her green eyes watched passively back at her from the mirror as she assessed her appearance. Just like every other day, she looked the same. Average height, average curves. Tanned skin—inevitable if you went around in shorts and tank tops all summer. And her latest look, dark shadows beneath her eyes.

In her workshop, her stereo played the latest country album, the massive doors of the stable were pinned back, and she'd opened all the windows, enjoying the summer day. A sheen of sweat covered her skin, and particles of sawdust stuck to her as she stripped back and repaired an old wardrobe. This was heaven on earth to Georgia, where she found peace and tranquility that calmed her busy mind.

At dusk, she packed away her tools and headed inside to shower. She pulled on a clean pair of jeans, a good pair of black cowboy boots, and a loose white cotton blouse. Her hair was still in its braid, and she'd made sure no bits of wood or sawdust was stuck in it. She slicked on some lip gloss and was good to go.

With her customary spin of wheels and stereo blasting, she peeled out of her driveway and headed north, towards the homestead farther up the road. They were far enough out of town that the road wasn't sealed, sending dust and loose gravel flying up from her tires. In a matter of minutes, she skidded to a halt in Zak's driveway and killed the engine. Jumping out of her truck, she smoothed suddenly sweaty palms against her denim-clad legs and approached the front door.

The wooden double doors had recently been painted a glossy black. Georgia pressed the doorbell and waited.

The door swung open, and Veronica ushered her inside.

"This is Frank." Veronica indicated the bulk of a man by her side. Also, a vampire, Georgia noted. Holy shit, what had she gotten herself into? She hoped she wasn't dinner.

Frank approached, his big bulky hands reaching out and frisking her before she could step away.

"What the fuck!" Georgia pulled back, outraged at having him touch her. "Hands off, buddy," she growled at him, her body unconsciously falling into a fighting stance.

Frank raised his hands, palms toward her in an apologetic manner, eyeing her warily.

"Rules. We've had trouble before. No weapons, no wires," he stated gruffly.

Georgia stretched her neck from side to side, letting her stance settle. She supposed security was a big concern for Zak; however, no one ever got frisked in a town like Redmeadows. And certainly not upon entering a home at the owner's invitation.

Annoyed, Georgia followed Veronica down a long hallway, building debris scattered around, the smell of sawdust lingering in the air. She was led to a large room that she guessed to be the formal dining room, judging by the massive dining table holding center court. The table was damaged, with scratches, gouges, and splits. A quick calculation and Georgia reckoned it would easily seat twenty people. Unfortunately, there weren't twenty matching chairs—there were a handful of mismatched kitchen chairs at one end. Seated at one of those chairs was Zak Goodwin himself.

He looked just like the photos on the back of his books. Hair as black as night, dark brows arching over equally dark eyes. Designer stubble across a strong, square jaw, full lips with a cupid's bow that made you want to trace your finger, or tongue, over it. Geez, the man was sex on legs, and Georgia wasn't immune. He radiated heat, and the earthy smell of elements, rich and potent, surrounded her.

He looked up as she approached, his dark eyes holding hers. Georgia sucked in a breath, the sheer presence of him stealing the air from her. She faltered for a moment, trying to feel him. He wasn't a vampire, but he was...something. She couldn't put her finger on it. What she could feel was the raw sexual magnetism that practically oozed from his pores. It washed over her in a sensual wave, like a warm caress. Shrugging the heady sensation off, she continued toward him, holding out her hand in greeting.

"Georgia Pearce."

He rose, his hand closing around hers, searing her flesh and sending tendrils of fire up her arm. Her hand tingled, and a familiar flash created spots before her eyes before images shimmered in her mind.

Zak lay on the rough stone ground, a knife buried up to the hilt in the center of his chest, the handle intricately carved with three ribbons entwined around the handle. A knife exactly like the one currently hidden in her farmhouse. Zak's eyes were open, staring lifelessly at nothing.

Within seconds the vision was over, and with a slight shake of her head Georgia shook off the residual disorientation that always followed. The color left her face when it clicked that she'd just witnessed his death. Should she say something? But what could you say, "Hey, I think I just saw you die? And by the way, I happen to own the knife that's going to ultimately end up sticking out of your chest." Yeah, right, hello, crazy lady.

"Thank you for coming. I'm Zak, but of course, you already knew that." He smiled self-deprecatingly, releasing her hand.

"Who doesn't? Your fangirls and the damn paparazzi have overrun our town!"

"Fangirls?" he drawled, tilting his head.

"You know the ones," she shrugged, "hanging around like they don't have a home to go to in the hopes of catching a glimpse of you, making a nuisance of themselves."

"A nuisance? Surely the influx of visitors to this town is good for business." Oh, but he had the sexiest accent; she found it hard to focus on what he was saying.

"It's helped a little," she admitted grudgingly, "if they took all the squealing and swooning down a few notches, it would almost be bearable. Getting asked a hundred times a day if I've seen you is getting old. Fast."

"So, you're not a fan?"

"On the contrary. I've read all your books. You tell a good tale, and I enjoy your stories, but..."

"But you don't feel the need to send me your underwear in the mail?" he guessed.

"I don't see the point," she agreed, "It wouldn't fit you. Kinda wasteful."

He laughed, "Can I get you a drink? Beer? Wine? Coffee?" he inquired, one dark brow arching.

"Coffee would be good."

His eyes left hers to settle on Veronica, who stood just behind Georgia's shoulder.

"Two coffees, thanks, Veronica."

He indicated that she pull up a chair next to him. Settling into her seat, Georgia released a shaky breath.

"Everything okay?"

"Sure. Just a bit nervous, to be honest," she lied, wiping her clammy palms on the legs of her jeans.

Zak frowned, his brows pinching together over dark eyes, and tilted his head to the side as if wondering what she was thinking.

His gaze dropped to her mouth, making it difficult to breathe, to concentrate.

"What are you?" His blunt question took her by surprise, and she looked at him, green eyes wide.

"What?"

"You're something more than human. Something happened just now when our hands touched. I felt your energy change. What was it? What did you do?"

"I've no idea what you're talking about," Georgia deflected. Fuck, how could he tell? Feel her energy change? What did *that* mean?

His hand reached up, spanning her jaw and tilting her face to his, studying her intently. Her skin burned from where he touched her. Shit, shit, shit, she was so busted!

A familiar tingling danced across her skin where his hand touched; a familiar heat swirled around her, sizzling her nerve endings and pooling low in her belly. Her eyes dropped to his lips, so close she only had to lean forward slightly, and they'd touch. And then she knew why he was so familiar.

"You're him," she said, her voice shakier than she'd have liked. "You visit my dreams. How is that possible?"

With infinite care, he slid his fingertips over her bottom lip, his expression intent.

"Sounds intriguing," he murmured, "tell me...how precisely do I manage to visit your dreams?"

Mesmerized, she watched him watching her. The touch of his fingers on her lips burnt a fiery trail, and she was *this close* to opening her mouth and touching him with her tongue.

Veronica broke the spell, returning with their drinks.

He released her, and she sank back in her chair, trying to orient herself. A cup of coffee was placed in front of her, and she busied herself adding sugar and milk, her eyes firmly on her cup while she stirred. She could feel Zak's stare but refused to meet his eyes again. Much to her relief, he let the matter drop. Pulling the iPad that lay on the table toward him, he showed her the floor plan of the house and told her of his plans for renovating the big old building.

He wanted her to build him a custom-made bed for the master bedroom.

"These are the kind of styles I like, but I'll leave the final design to you." Leaning forward, he showed her a half dozen pictures on his iPad. Flicking through them, he looked up, eyes pinning her in place. "Think you can manage that?"

"Definitely." She nodded, jumping a little when he slapped his palm on the table top. "And this? I'd like it restored."

"It's a beauty," she breathed, running her hand over the old timber.

"I'll need chairs too. Twenty."

"Of course."

When he revealed how much he was willing to

pay her for the custom bed and dining table restoration, Georgia knew there was no way she could turn him down. It would pay the mortgage on the farm and the lease on the shop (and Skye's apartment) for the next six months.

"Just so you know, he's mine."

Georgia had been opening the door of her truck, getting ready to leave, when Veronica's words stopped her. She looked at the other woman over her shoulder.

"Excuse me?"

"Oh, you can play your eye fuck games all you like," Veronica sneered, "and he probably will fuck you 'cos you're fresh meat, but I thought it only fair to warn you that, seriously..." she eyed Georgia up and down with disdain, "you'll only hold his interest for a heartbeat. Once he gets you to spread your legs, his interest in you will end." She spoke crudely, and it made Georgia's flesh crawl.

"He's mine. He'll use you and be back in my bed before you know it."

"And that doesn't bother you?" Georgia

challenged, "That you can't keep his interest enough to stay faithful to you?"

Veronica tensed, her hands curling into fists. "That's what he loves about me. I allow him to take other lovers, and he allows the same of me. Sometimes we bring these lovers into our bed and share the fun. But no matter who he fucks, he *always* returns to my bed."

Georgia felt sick at the mental image of Zak rolling around in bed with Veronica, and God knows who else.

"We've been together many years," Veronica continued, voice cutting, "I know him like no other woman, and only I can give him what he needs. What he really needs."

"Whatever." Georgia shrugged, faking a casualness she didn't feel and climbed into her truck, wheels spinning and the stereo blasting. *Psycho bitch.*

CHAPTER
FIVE

Zak listened to the roar of Georgia's truck as she left.

"What a woman." She intrigued him. She was the reason he had moved to the other side of the world. When the dagger, the first blade, had activated his ring, he'd traced it. It had brought him to her doorstep.

He'd managed to infiltrate her dreams, but not her mind. The first night he'd visited her sleep, he hadn't been prepared for the surge of desire that had flamed between them. He'd never felt anything like it. It was as if the fires of hell had consumed him, burning him to his very soul. He hadn't been able to stop himself from returning night after night, her warm flesh tempting him, her soft lips moaning as she'd writhed beneath him, begging for release.

She was more potent in the flesh. She appeared wanton and gorgeous in person, and Zak had trouble catching his breath. He'd managed to stop himself from throwing her onto the dining table and sheathing himself in her. Just. It had taken a considerable amount of control. Such sensations were foreign to him. He usually took what he wanted, when he wanted it. Georgia was different. He didn't want to just take from her; he wanted her to give.

"Well?" Frank asked from the doorway.

"She's an enigma. I can't read her." In five hundred years, there had never been a mind he couldn't enter, read their thoughts, play with their memories or even wipe a mind clean if he so desired. Except for Georgia Pearce.

Frank chuckled at the stunned look on his face, enjoying seeing his boss so rattled. "Why do you think that is?" he asked

Zak shrugged. "I'm pretty sure she's a seer. But even so, I've met seers before and been able to read them."

"Could it be because she awoke the blade? That it has some power over her?"

"I don't know. But I'm going to find out." No matter how attractive he found her, no matter how the burning need to possess her was ever-present, it did nothing to explain how a seer who was able to block him happened to end up activating the first blade. He didn't believe in coincidence or chance. There was more to Georgia Pearce, and he was determined to find out exactly what it was.

THE FOLLOWING morning Georgia drove over to Zak's place, iPad and tape measure on the seat beside her. She'd spent the evening nutting out a few concepts for the master bedroom and had transferred them to her iPad to show Zak.

Designing the bed had kept her mind off the man himself. However, it was a double-edged sword considering it was his bed she was fantasizing over. For the first time in a month, he didn't visit her dreams, but that didn't stop her from dreaming of him, of the feelings he aroused in her. She'd tossed and turned as she'd dreamt of his hands on her, then the unwelcome presence of Veronica in their bed, touching him. He'd rolled from her and into the other woman's arms, and Georgia had wanted to cry. The dream had ended with the vision of him dead, and she'd woken in a panic, heart thundering in her chest.

She knew her visions weren't set in stone; they were only accurate when she viewed them. People changed their minds, their actions, and that, in turn, could change future events. That's why Georgia didn't like to reveal her visions very often. If people didn't like what they heard, they took action to avoid it, but sometimes, that action led to the same result. Fate could be a bitch.

Frank met her at the door this time and let her in —she eyeballed him as he took a step toward her, then quickly stepped back without frisking.

"That's more like it," she grumbled, clipping her tape measure to her shorts pocket and clasping her iPad to her chest.

"Is Zak around? I've got an idea for his bedroom."

"I'm all for hearing about bedroom ideas," he spoke from behind her.

"Jesus!" she gasped, clutching a hand to her chest in fright, "Do you always sneak up behind people?"

"I wouldn't call it sneaking when I'm in my own

home," he commented. His gaze was as intense as she remembered it.

"I've got a concept for your bed, plus I need to measure up properly."

"This way," with a sweeping gesture, he indicated the staircase in the foyer. Georgia preceded him up the stairs, acutely aware of him behind her.

He showed her to an empty room.

"Let's see what you've got."

"What?" she gasped, spinning to face him.

"Your design? Don't you want to show me?" His grin told her he knew exactly where her mind was, and it wasn't on interior design.

"Oh. Yes. Of course." She'd been standing in the middle of the room, looking around, but came back to him where he leaned against the doorframe. He straightened to look at her iPad, standing so close their hips touched.

He didn't speak, and Georgia started to feel nervous. Shit, he hated it. Damn, she'd never had anyone hate her designs before.

"This is perfect, Georgia," he finally said. "It's more than I was expecting."

"Oh, do you think it'll cost too much? I could possibly source a cheaper wood."

"You misunderstand. Money is no object," that dimple appeared in his cheek again, "The level of detail, the design is so unique."

A blush heated her cheeks. She had designed the bed for him—the sexy hero in her dreams, the mysterious hero in his books, the fantasy that her imagination insisted on spinning around him, no matter how much she told herself to cut it out. She didn't know how to respond, so she kept silent.

"This one, definitely." He touched the iPad. "I'll transfer half the funds into your account today so you can order what you need, the remaining half on completion. Email me an invoice or your bank details or something." He turned to leave, suddenly business-like.

"Ok."

"Ooops, forgot—got something for you." He spun back to her, clasping her hand in his and leading her across the room to two doors. Opening one of the doors, he flicked the light switch to the windowless room—obviously intended to be a walk-in closet. On the floor were boxes containing top-of-the-line power tools, chisels, hammers, handsaws, basically a carpenter's wet dream.

"For you." He indicated the tools. "Since I'll need

you to work on-site, it makes sense for you to have a set of tools here at your disposal."

Her mouth was hanging open. "This is too much," she whispered, turning to him, her eyes shining.

"Want to show your appreciation?" he leered at her, crowding her.

Exasperated, she pushed him back. *What is it with men and one-track minds?*

"I'm not one of your conquests," she muttered, pissed at him for ruining the moment. She wanted to get her hands on the exquisite tools he'd bought for her; now, he was the tool.

"You could be," he offered, his expression hopeful.

"Pft. In your dreams." She stomped away from him, setting up to measure where she wanted the bed to go.

"You're already in my dreams, sweetheart," she heard as he left the room, leaving her flustered and flushed.

Back at home later that afternoon, Georgia had just finished helping the local courier guys load a desk, kitchen dresser, and rocking chair into the back of their truck and was standing outside of her workshop, stretching when another truck turned into her drive. On the back of the tray was Zak's dining table. Following the truck was a familiar yellow Jeep, Zak behind the wheel.

"Hey guys," Georgia called to the crew, ignoring him. She wasn't sure exactly WHY she was angry with him, just that she was. It shouldn't bother her in the least that he was getting his jollies with the stunning Veronica, but somehow...it mattered. And she didn't like it, not one bit.

The work crew made lifting the massive table off the back of the truck and into her workshop look effortless, as if it weighed nothing. She'd cleared space in the center of the workshop for the dining table, allowing plenty of room to work from any angle.

Dressed again in her worn shorts and stained tank top, she kept her back to Zak, standing with her hands on her hips as she eyed the table and mentally plotting out her plan of attack. Strip it back first, of course, but then she'd need to get the splits fixed, then sand back the dings and dents. Rather than a rustic effect, she wanted this table to be sleek, smooth, and perfect.

A finger traced down the inside of her upper arm. She snatched her arm away, stepping away from Zak.

"What does your tattoo say?"

Her tattoo was hard to see on the inside of her upper arm.

"What does it matter to you?" She was still annoyed at him for hitting on her. It was one thing to have a hot guy hit on you, but when he already had a girlfriend? What an asshole. Worse was that she had the hots for him. Her own guilt at wanting someone who was already taken notched her anger up.

"Doesn't," he shrugged, "just curious. I didn't notice it before."

"It's private."

"There are other places you could have put it on your body where it wouldn't be seen." His eyes raked her body, lingering on her breasts.

"Oh fuck off," she snapped, striding away, inexplicably furious.

"Hey," he followed her as she stomped up the path towards the farmhouse, "what's crawled up your butt?"

"Seriously?" Eyes spitting fire, she planted her palm against his chest and shoved him, forcing him to take a step back. Little did she know it wasn't often anyone got away with pushing Zak Goodwin;

she didn't realize how much slack he was cutting her.

Georgia's temper was simmering, and when it blew, well, she hit things, or threw things, or broke something. Whenever her temper got the better of her, she got physical and look out whoever stood in her way when that happened. Zak either didn't heed the warning or chose to ignore it. With a finger, he poked her in the shoulder in return, "Seriously."

"You're an A-class wanker, you know that?" she spat.

"I've been called worse," he drawled, "but it would be kinda nice to know why you're slinging shit at me."

"Fuck you! I'm not playing your games, so just leave me the hell alone."

"There are all sorts of games I'd like to play with you, Georgia. Give me a hint here."

"Does Veronica know what a man whore you are?" she demanded.

"Veronica?" He appeared genuinely puzzled.

"Yeah, you know, tall blonde lives with you? Ring any bells?"

"Veronica is my personal assistant, Georgia," he explained patiently. "Veronica lives in my house, yes, but we're not a couple."

"You're not?" Georgia's eyebrows couldn't possibly have climbed any further up her forehead.

"No," he chuckled, "I haven't been in a relationship for a VERY long time."

"Bullshit. Your face is always splashed around on the internet, dating bimbo after bimbo."

"I don't do relationships, but I do have sex. Often."

"So you're telling me you're a one-night-stand kinda guy?"

"Sometimes it's more than one night," he shrugged, "if the sex is good and the lady willing, I'll stick around for a while."

"So you ARE a man-whore."

"Have you lived your life so perfectly you've earned the right to judge me?" He threw up his hands in exasperation, turning away from her and heading for his jeep.

"You jerk!" she shouted after him, "I quit. Call your fucking team to get your fucking table and clear the fuck out!" Anger sizzled through her veins like lava, burning, twisting, poisoning.

"No, you don't." He started the engine and drove off before she could reply, leaving her standing with her cheeks flushed, hands on her hips, glaring at the jeep as it disappeared down her driveway.

CHAPTER
SIX

What's wrong with me?

Georgia straightened the swinging punching bag, steadying it ready for another round of her unrelenting fists. She'd had anger issues in her teens but had learned to keep a handle on it once she was an adult. Today Zak reduced her to a hormonal teenager within minutes. And she didn't like it, not one bit.

Thump, thump, thump. Left, right, jab, kick. Her heart thumped against her ribs. Her muscles burned from the strain. She'd been laying into the bag for over an hour, landing punch after punch, kick after kick, trying to eradicate the pent-up energy of her anger.

Thump, thump, thump. Why? Why did he get

under her skin? Why did she even care who he was sleeping with? She didn't. Punch. *Liar.* Punch. It wasn't like her to judge; hell, when she had an itch that needed scratching, she didn't hesitate to find someone willing and able. She didn't date, so why the double standard when it came to Zak doing the same?

Gasping for breath, she stepped back and, leaning forward with her hands on her knees, she drew in great gulps of air, her lungs burning. Sweat dripped from her forehead, making small raindrop shapes on the ground. The buzzing of her phone was a welcome distraction.

Straightening, she grabbed her towel, blotted at her face, and snatched up her phone.

"Skye Blue," she puffed out.

"Hey! Caught you at a bad time?"

"Working out."

"Sounds intense. You're really puffing."

"Punching the shit out of the punching bag. Soothing."

"Who pissed you off?" Skye recognized the signs.

"Doesn't matter. I'll deal."

"Let me know if I can help." Skye's voice was

gentle. She knew Georgia hated the battle she had with her temper. How it had gotten so bad as a teenager, she'd almost landed in juvy. That it had been a constant source of friction between Georgia and their father, a law enforcement officer. How many times he'd had to bail her ass out of trouble, stop charges from being laid 'cos she'd lost her cool. Skye still remembered the shouting matches between the pair.

"Will do. What's up?"

"Tomorrow's the anniversary. I'm going to the cemetery...you in?"

Georgia closed her eyes against the sudden sweep of pain that threatened to crush her. Another year already? That made six years. Six years since her parents had died in that senseless car crash. Six years since she'd failed them.

"I'm in. What time?"

"Sunset. Seven o'clock. Mom loved the sunset."

"I'll meet you there." Georgia hung up, her chest tight. Six years wiped away as if it had been yesterday. Everyone told her it would get easier, that time would heal, so why did she still feel so raw? Why did it still hurt so damn much?

"Fuck it," she growled, dropping the towel to the floor and heading inside.

"ANOTHER ROUND, EDDIE!" Slamming her glass on the bar Georgia eyeballed the bartender. *Just try and cut me off. I dare you.*

Another double scotch, no ice, appeared in front of her. She tossed a handful of cash on the bar before slamming down the contents in one gulp. The alcohol burned down her throat, but she barely noticed.

"I'll pour you another one, but only if you promise to take it slow." Eddie frowned at her.

Fine. Whatever. Bloody pussies, the lot of 'em.

"Deal." She took a mouthful but stopped herself from downing the entire contents in one gulp. Instead, she set the glass down carefully in front of her, staring down into the amber contents as if they could reveal the secrets of the universe.

Satisfied that she'd keep her word and slow down, Eddie moved off to serve other patrons. The noise in the bar washed over her, seemingly muted, as if she was underwater. She wasn't sure if it resulted from the alcohol or the grief pouring through her, as fresh today as it had been six years ago.

As promised, she'd met Skye at the cemetery, a

fragrant bouquet of pink lilies in her hand. Her mother's favorite. Skye had brought yellow daisies for their dad. The girls laid the fresh flowers on the graves, side by side.

"It's okay to forgive yourself," Skye had told her, clasping her hand as they stood in front of the graves.

"Don't."

"Georgia...it wasn't your fault. It was an accident. Just a stupid accident."

"I should have seen it. I should have been able to stop it from happening. I could have told them to take a different route that night or not go out at all."

"Please don't do this to yourself," Skye had begged, hating the pain and anguish in her sister's eyes. "How could you have seen a car crash? A single moment in time, water on the road making it slippery?"

"They should be here, Skye!" Pulling away from her, she spun, heading back to her car, needing to drown the pain, to dull the sharp edges that stabbed at her.

"HEY BEAUTIFUL, COME HERE OFTEN?"

"Really? That's your pickup line?" Georgia eyed the idiot who'd just slid onto the bar stool next to her.

"Actually, it wasn't a pickup line," he lied, "but a serious question. So? Do you?"

"I'm really not in the mood." She turned back to her drink. The idiot wasn't that bad looking, she supposed: blonde, blue-eyed, nice build, muscular shoulders.

"I bet I could get you in the mood," he purred, running a finger down her arm.

Seriously?

"I'm going to say this slowly, so you understand. Don't. Touch. Me. I'm not interested. Now go away." She shrugged away from his touch.

The idiot took no heed, raising his hand to brush the back of his fingers across her cheek, leaning in close to whisper in her ear, "You...me...naked...."

"Okay, I'm telling you twice. Don't touch me. Ever. Understood?"

His hand trailed down her cheek to her collarbone. Reaching up, she snatched his hand with hers, squeezing painfully.

"I've asked you twice. Agreed? Eddie, you're a witness here. I asked him, twice, not to touch me, didn't I?"

"You did," Eddie agreed.

"Ok then."

A loud crack, and he was lying on the floor, blood streaming from his nose. The sting in her knuckles told her that she'd nailed him a good one. Idiot. Without another glance, she turned back to her drink, closing her eyes and letting the alcohol swirl around her tongue.

She sensed movement around her as his mates helped him to his feet, heard his muttered "bitch," as they led him away, but she paid them no heed.

"Eddie," she called. The bartender leaned toward her, a slow grin on his face.

"You did good there," he told her. "You didn't pummel him into next week."

"Must be slipping." She grinned back. "Eddie, you know what?" she slurred, the effects of the scotch kicking in.

"What?"

"I think I'm going to call it a night."

"Really? No dancing on the bar tonight?" he teased.

"Not tonight. Tonight I shall try and be rethsponshible. For mom and dad," her words thick and heavy.

"Want me to call a cab? Or Rhys?" Eddie offered.

"Neither!" she declared, sliding from the bar stool and steadying herself against the bar with one hand when the room swayed. "I'm going to walk."

"Walk?" Eddie laughed. "Georgia, you live miles away. Too far to walk, girl," he chided.

"Nevertheless..." and off she sauntered, weaving her way to the door.

"I'll call Rhys," Eddie muttered.

Outside, the fresh air sobered her somewhat, and she took a moment, leaning against the outside of the building, to study the star-filled sky. Were her parents up there now, looking down on her? Proud of what she'd made of her life? Or still shaking their heads at her, wanting her to do better? She hoped her dad wasn't angry that she'd punched the idiot. She'd done what he'd taught her. Ask them twice. Make sure you ask them twice and then hit them. *See dad? I remembered.*

Georgia successfully avoided Zak for three days. Rhys had turned up to question her over the assault at the bar. No charges were pressed, and she supposed she should be grateful, but Georgia couldn't bring herself to care. Of course, she'd been busted leaving the police station, and the local rag had posted a status update about her on Facebook, along with a picture of her scowling and flipping the bird to the camera.

Skye had texted her, "It's ok, I'm not mad. Rhys filled me in."

Zak texted her, "Everything ok?"

She ignored both. That is until the timber

arrived for Zak's bed, and she had no choice but to face him.

Face like a thundercloud, she climbed the steps to his front door and rang the doorbell. Frank let her in, handing her a key.

"Might as well let yourself in in the future," he told her before disappearing towards the back of the house. Slipping the key onto her keyring, Georgia headed straight upstairs to the master bedroom and got to work.

She didn't see any sign of Zak all morning and had successfully managed to put him out of her mind by the time he showed up in the afternoon.

"Is it safe to come in?" he asked from the doorway. Georgia turned off the bandsaw, pulling her dust mask down around her neck and her protective earmuffs and goggles onto the top of her head.

"You need something?"

"I need all sorts of things," he insinuated. Sighing in frustration, Georgia glared at him.

"Can't you ever be serious? Does everything always have to be a come-on with you?" she grumbled.

"I can be serious," he told her, "deadly serious."

With a deadpan face, he moved toward her, stopping within arm's reach.

"Seriously, Zak, you give me a headache. Can't you just leave me alone to get this job done, and I can get out of your hair?"

"What if I like you in my hair? In my house. In my bed...room."

Slipping her safety equipment back over her face, she turned the saw back on, ignoring him. Sawdust flew, and the saw whined as it ate through the timber she fed it. She didn't hear him leave the room but felt it when he'd left the radius of her senses. The tension slowly eased from her shoulders, and she focused on her work, blocking all thoughts of the sexy celebrity from her mind. At five, she heard the mass exodus of the construction crew, and, not keen to be left in the house alone, she packed up for the day, escaping without seeing anyone.

She'd arranged to meet Skye at the gym after work, and they'd made plans to grab a bite to eat afterward. She stopped in at the farmhouse to change into her gym gear and pack a bag with a change of clothes—she'd shower and change at the gym after her workout.

"Hey Georgie Girl," Skye was standing outside the gym when she pulled up.

Georgia teased back, pulling her sister in for a hug, "Skye Blue." The aerobics class had already started, so they decided to do their own routine on the bikes and treadmill.

"How's it going with Zak Goodwin?" Skye asked as they sat side by side on stationary bikes, leg pumping as they peddled to nowhere.

"I'll be glad when it's over," Georgia admitted, "Zak Goodwin might be sex on legs, but he's got an ego to go with it," she grumbled.

"Oh? What happened?"

"Oh, nothing really, he just hits on me all the time."

"Geez, Georgie, you must be the only woman on this earth who'd complain about having Zak Goodwin hit on them."

"Hate to burst your bubble, Skye—he's made it very clear he's a love 'em and leave 'em type of guy. While he didn't come out and say, 'let's have no strings attached sex', that's the vibe I got. And I'm not interested in becoming another notch on his bedpost."

"Oh yuk. Creep," Skye agreed. "Rhys called into

the shop today, asked if we wanted to see the band playing at the pub this weekend."

"Yeah? That'd be cool. You in?"

"I guess. I don't want to be the third wheel, though."

"Errr, hang on a minute, genius. He came in asking YOU. Why would that make you the third wheel? If anything, I'd be the third wheel."

"Maybe he asked me first because he saw me before he saw you. It's you he's interested in."

"I wouldn't be so sure of that, Skye."

"Seriously, Georgia, how can you not see he's got the hots for you?" Skye protested.

"I think he's confused. Don't get me wrong, I think he's the perfect guy, the perfect catch, but he's in my friend zone. I don't want to lose that. If we try something and it doesn't work, I'll have lost a dear, dear friend. A friend I really don't want to lose."

"You're not having much luck with men these days, are you?" Skye commented, switching to the treadmill, making chitchat difficult.

Wrapping up their workout, the girls showered, then hit the local pizza parlor before Georgia headed home around nine. She'd had a good night. She and Skye were close. Their parents had died when Skye was eighteen and Georgia twenty. It had brought the sisters closer than ever.

They'd used the small inheritance to get the shop started and as a down payment on the farm. Skye had lived with Georgia for a while, but she hadn't liked living so far out of town, and they'd decided to do up the apartment above the shop for her.

Skidding to a halt out in front of the farmhouse, Georgia climbed out of the truck and took a moment to enjoy the star-studded sky. She turned and made her way to the front door with a happy sigh. She'd unlocked it and was just pushing it open when her senses fired, and someone made their presence known by pushing her in the middle of the back, sending her sprawling across the floor. The front door clicked shut ominously behind her.

Picking herself up and dusting herself off, she turned to face her foe. Blue jeans, faded red t-shirt, well built, solid. His hair was closely shaved to his scalp, and the bulging arms crossed over his chest were covered in tattoos. All in all, a very scary-looking vampire. Too bad she'd only felt him a second before he attacked.

"My boss has a job for you," he told her.

"Sorry, I'm all booked up. He'll have to look elsewhere."

She didn't see him move. She did, however, feel his hand grab her by the throat and shove her back into the wall. Her training kicked in. Her dad had brought his girls up never to be the victim.

Swinging her forearm up, she dislodged his grip with her right arm while delivering a cracking blow to his nose with her left. He let go, both hands going to his nose, which was streaming blood. She brought her knee up into his groin, hard. When he doubled over, groaning, she delivered another forceful punch to his stomach, putting everything she had into it.

Hoping she'd bought herself enough time, she rushed to the front door. She wasn't foolish enough to believe she could outfight a vampire, but if she could buy herself enough time to get in her truck and get away, that was a win in her books.

She wasn't fast enough. The vamp pulled himself together by the time she reached the front door—a mere three seconds later. With an outraged snarl, he lunged for her back. She half-turned, managing to get a leg up, her boot landing against his stomach to try and hold him off. He grabbed her ankle and twisted, pain shooting up her leg and forcing her to rotate her body in the same direction or risk him snapping her bones.

She found herself face down on the floor, one furious vampire sitting on her back, crushing her.

"Listen up, bitch," he snarled in her ear. With no other options open to her at that moment, Georgia complied.

"Zak Goodwin has a ring. My boss needs it. You've got one week to deliver the ring. Before you protest again, know this—I not only know where you live, I know where your sister lives. Understand me?" Georgia's heart froze at the apparent threat to her sister. "Understand?" He shook her when she didn't respond. She nodded her head, unable to draw breath to speak with him crushing her lungs.

"One week. I'll be watching. Tell anyone about this, and your sister gets it." His hand wound into her braid, pulling her head back before slamming her forehead into the floor. Pain exploded behind her eyes then everything went black.

Georgia wasn't sure how much time had passed before she came to. She struggled to a sitting position, a hand going to her forehead where she could feel a huge lump. Her head throbbed, and she knew she'd have a wicked bruise. Feeling shaky, she clambered to her feet. Making her way into the kitchen, she searched for an ice pack to put on the swollen lump on her forehead and some painkillers.

On the fridge door, a photo was stuck beneath a magnet. It was a picture of a ring—she assumed it was the ring Zak had that these goons wanted. She squinted closer at the design woven into the band. Wait... it was the same design as the dagger, only on a smaller scale. How could that be? Scrawled across the bottom corner of the photo were the words, "I'm watching."

Head hurting too much to think of the mess she'd managed to find herself in, Georgia shoved the photo into a drawer.

After taking some painkillers, she slowly climbed the stairs, holding a bag of frozen peas against her aching head. In the bathroom, she turned on the taps to the bath, knowing she would be sore tomorrow. Her hip ached where the vamp had twisted her leg, and her ribs felt bruised where she'd hit the floor, and he'd sat on her. Thankfully she didn't think anything was broken.

As the bath filled, she examined her injury in the mirror. The skin hadn't broken, but a bruise was already forming. Despite the swelling, she'd probably gotten off lucky. Stripping off, she eased her aching bones into the soothing water, settling back with a sigh, for once in her trouble-strewn life at a loss as to what to do.

Even if she wanted to, she didn't know how she'd get the ring away from Zak. She'd have to watch to see if he ever took it off. But then what? How would she steal it out from under him? It crossed her mind that she could simply tell him about the vamp's visit, but could she risk her sister's safety? Would the vamp find out and hurt her sister before Zak could do anything about it? And there was no guarantee Zak would protect her sister or even be inclined to do anything about the vamp who'd visited her. It wasn't a risk she was prepared to take.

THERE WAS no hiding that bruise, Georgia admitted the following morning. The unattractive lump had gone down, leaving a dark bruise the size of her palm, reaching from her eyebrow to her hairline. She'd considered styling her hair differently to try and hide it, but there was no way, so she pulled her hair back into a high ponytail instead, letting it swing down her back.

She'd just let herself into Zak's house, hoping to

get upstairs to the bedroom before anyone saw her, but her luck had clearly run out. Zak himself was moving down the hallway from the back of the house, coffee cup in hand.

"Morning, want a cup?" He indicated his mug.

"No, I'm good, thanks," Georgia kept moving, but he intercepted her at the bottom of the stairs. His free hand grabbed her arm.

"You're hurt."

"Just a bruise. I'm fine." She tried to shrug his hand off her arm, but he held on. He turned her to face him fully.

"Who did it?" he growled, anger darkening his eyes.

"Geez, settle down," she complained, not meeting his eyes, "no one 'did it'" her fingers using air quotes, "I tripped and smacked my head into the door frame. No big deal."

He knew she was lying. Her heart was racing, and she refused to look at him.

"No, you didn't."

"Leave it." She took off up the stairs, hoping he wouldn't notice her limp. Her leg and hip were still painful from the twist and fall, and her ribs ached with each breath. She let out a sigh of relief when he didn't follow her.

Work was hell. Each movement caused her injuries to flare in protest. She was kneeling on the floor, laying out the basic framework for the bed, pain radiating through her body. With a groan, she straightened. God, she felt like crap. It was time for another dose of painkillers.

Before she could get the strip of pain killers out of her back pocket, Zak came striding into the room, determination in every step.

"That's it," he snapped, hauling her to her feet. She cried out, her muscles protesting at the sudden movement. "I've been feeling your pain all morning. This is more than a bump on the head. What the fuck is going on, Georgia!" His anger made her bristle.

"Oh, stop trying to be the hero," she scolded. "This isn't one of your books."

He closed his eyes with an exasperated sigh. "Christ, woman."

Georgia swayed before him, her hand reaching out to steady herself against his chest. Her body hurt everywhere—she'd pushed herself too hard today with her injuries, and she was paying the price.

He pulled her into his arms, and she struggled, causing more pain.

"Let me go," she whispered, pain making her

fragile, and she hated it. It hurt so much she thought she was going to be sick. Maybe she had some broken bones after all.

"The longer you struggle, the longer I hold you," he murmured. She stopped struggling, and he smiled. "Relax."

The air changed. She swore she could see a white glow, like an aura surrounding them. His warm palm rested against her bruised brow before slowly moving down, seemingly knowing where she was hurt and heading straight to her sore spots, laying against her ribs, then her hip. Each place he touched flared with a sharp, hot sting followed by a strange tingling sensation, the pain slowly easing before disappearing altogether.

She felt dizzy and slightly sick, her knees giving way beneath her. He supported her weight, moving them across the floor before sliding down the wall until he was seated on the floor, positioning her on his lap, her back resting against his chest, her head falling back on his shoulder.

Georgia knew she should protest, but she simply didn't have the energy to move. He'd done something to her. Her bones felt like limp strands of spaghetti, but at least the pain was gone.

"You've healed me," she murmured.

"I have." His voice rumbled against her back.

"You're not a vampire. You would have healed me with blood."

"You know about vampires?" He sounded surprised.

"I know about all sorts of creatures," she admitted, "have ever since I was a kid."

"That explains it." He absently stroked her arm. "You're psychic?" he guessed.

"Mmmm." Her eyes drifted closed. Whatever spell he was weaving around them was working. She was sleepy, relaxed, more comfortable than she cared to admit. She'd just steal a few minutes, she told herself.

"You're something...just can't get a read on you," she admitted.

"Well, you're half right. I'm a half-breed. Half-vampire, half angel."

Georgia's eyes opened, and she turned to look at him, not lifting her head from his shoulder. She wasn't surprised by his admission. Or afraid. He looked down at her. Their faces were so close their lips were practically touching, his dark eyes burning into hers. He was so goddamn sexy.

She felt something pushing at her mind and squinted her eyes at him.

"What are you doing?"

"Trying to read your mind."

"Is it working?" God, why was she so lethargic? She knew she should be angry at him for the intrusion, yet she couldn't seem to stir herself to react.

"No. For some reason, I can't read you."

"That's good."

"You're the only one I can't read."

"Ever?"

"Ever." She watched him, watching her. Her eyes drifted closed as his mouth lowered to hers. He was like a drug, affecting her senses, clouding her mind. Softly his mouth touched hers, his lips warm. A sigh drifted from her, and he took advantage, easing her lips open, seeking access to her mouth. She gave it up without a second thought. Mouth moving against his, getting hungrier by the second, her tongue dueling with his.

The hand on her arm moved up to her neck, sliding against her jaw and cupping the back of her head, holding her in place while his mouth plundered hers. She could feel his erection grow against her hip, her core tightening in response.

Breathless, she broke the kiss, panting.

"I can't."

"Why fight it? I know you want me just as badly as I want you." His growled words sent a shudder of arousal through her. She needed to put some distance between them so she could think straight.

Before he could stop her, she'd crawled off his lap, kneeling on the floor several feet away, not sure her legs would support her if she tried to stand. He let her go, raising one knee and resting his arm on it as he regarded her.

"Who roughed you up last night? An old boyfriend?"

Oh, so they were back to that. The change of topic was a relief.

"No one. I told you, I did it to myself. Anyway, why old boyfriend? Could be a current boyfriend."

"You're a lousy liar. And I asked around. There's no boyfriend."

"You asked around? Why?" She scooted further away until she was leaning against the opposite wall, the length of the room between them.

"I'd prefer not to have the complication of a jealous boyfriend when I fuck you."

"You're not going to fuck me!" she protested.

"It's inevitable, Georgia. But in the meantime, I can help you with this." His hand waved at her body, indicating the injuries he'd just healed.

"You can't help." She chose to ignore his outrageous claim that he would get her into bed. One kiss didn't mean anything.

"Try me. You'd be surprised."

Georgia considered for a moment. Could she put her sister in jeopardy? Would the vamp who'd paid her a visit somehow know if she told Zak? No, she couldn't risk it.

"I can't. Just leave it." Scrambling to her feet, Georgia quickly left the room. It would be so easy to tell him, but there were no guarantees it wouldn't make matters worse. His house in Elen Hills had just been blown to kingdom come for Christ's sake; obviously, trouble was following him around, and somehow, she'd been dragged into it.

"Fuck it," she heard him curse as she rushed down the stairs. Spending the rest of the day working on the dining table in her workshop seemed the best option for now.

ZAK HEARD the front door slam, followed seconds later by the roar of Georgia's truck.

He sat where she'd left him, the taste of her still on his lips. He'd never had to work at getting a woman into bed before; hell, they'd been throwing themselves at his feet for the past five hundred years.

He was riled and frustrated. He was inexplicably drawn to her, the effect she had on him unsettling. He wanted her, badly, burned with the need to have her surrender to him, but there was something else. He was concerned for her, angry that someone had hurt her, disappointed that she wouldn't confide in him. He'd find out who'd laid hands on her and destroy the bastard. No one touched what was his. He was also unsettled by the powerful emotions he hadn't experienced in years, if ever.

While he couldn't read Georgia's mind, he could read her body. He knew she wanted him, but he also knew something had her on edge and distracted. She projected such a tough girl image that she could handle anyone and anything that came her way, but he was starting to see the cracks, and if she'd only let him help her, he could spare her all this unnecessary stress.

He also needed to find out what she knew about the first blade.

Georgia pulled off a boxing glove with her teeth, body covered in a sheen of sweat, breath rasping in and out of her chest. The bag had taken a fair beating this evening. She'd tried to work off her frustrations on the dining table, but nothing could shake the memory of the kiss she'd shared with Zak—and his certainty that they were destined to take things further. But what rattled her most was his unspoken concern for her, the way he'd held her after he'd healed her, the comfort she felt coming off him in waves.

She'd just pulled off her other boxing glove when a sound outside caught her attention. She focused, searching with her mind. There! A faint tingling. A vampire was approaching. With no time to think, she quickly palmed a chisel from the workbench, the blade resting along the inside of her arm, out of sight. Seconds later, the thug appeared in the workshop doorway. Surprise briefly shot across his face when he saw her unbruised face.

"Well, well, well," he murmured, walking toward her. She refused to back away. He was trying to intimidate her, and even though it was working, he didn't need to know that.

"This is going to be easier than we thought." He stopped in front of her and reached out to touch her face. She jerked her head away, which he ignored. "He's healed you." He watched her for a moment, thinking.

"Unless..." he suddenly grasped her by the throat and propelled her back against the wall, "unless you told him about my visit?" he snarled.

"If I'd told him, do you think you'd be standing here now?" she replied, as calmly as she could, even though her heart was thundering in her chest. "He'd have torn this town apart looking for you." Georgia didn't know if that was true; Zak may shrug and not give a damn, but she was going on instinct here.

The thug grunted in acknowledgment. "You've seen the ring?" he demanded.

"He wears it. I don't know how you think I'm

meant to get it away from him without him noticing. It's not like I can ask him for it, and he'll simply hand it over."

"Find a way," he snarled, backhanding her across the face. The force of the blow knocked her off her feet. Eyes watering from the sting in her cheek, she flipped the blade in her hand and lunged for him, sinking the sharp blade into his abdomen. She'd been aiming for his chest, hopefully, his heart, but he'd moved, and she'd struck much lower than intended.

He roared in pain. She kept a grip on the chisel while they both struggled for it. It weakened him; if she could just get another shot, she might be able to take this asshole out. It was too hard to try and drag the chisel up through his torso, she wasn't strong enough, but if she pulled it out and then rammed it back in a few inches higher, that'd do it.

She pulled it out and had it raised in both hands, this time above his heart, but those precious few seconds were all the vamp needed. Still bleeding heavily, he pushed her away and fled.

Georgia brushed the dirt off her backside and assessed her injuries. Besides the sting in her cheek and the bruising on her neck, she'd actually come out of this round okay. Not bad for a human chick.

ZAK WAS WAITING for her as she pulled up the following morning. He stepped down the porch and was at the door of her truck before she'd turned off the engine. She pushed the door open, forcing him to step back.

"Geez, Zak, a bit of space, please," she grumbled at him. Hands clamping down on her shoulders kept her from moving as his eyes did a thorough inspection of her body. Her cheek had been a little pink this morning, but tinted moisturizer had taken care of that. Unfortunately, the finger and thumbprints circling her throat hadn't been so easy to cover up. He spotted them immediately, his own hand spanning her throat, measuring the bruises— only his touch was feather-soft against her skin.

"Someone grabbed you by the throat, hard enough to bruise."

There was no lie to get her out of it, so she said nothing. His hand moved up to touch her cheek.

"And you're hiding something here." His thumb stroked across her cheek, and she closed her eyes, not wanting to enjoy the caress but unable to help herself.

"Who is hurting you?" he asked softly, so close

she could feel his breath against her face. She didn't dare open her eyes. If she looked into the depths of his, she might give in, and she didn't want that; she could handle this on her own. She'd gotten rid of the thug vamp last night with minimal injury to herself —she could do it again. If they found out she'd told him, they'd hurt Skye.

With a soft curse, he stepped back. Clasping her hand in his, he entwined their fingers. Her eyes shot open. He was grinning at her.

"Coffee?" Confused and wary of his change of tactic, she nodded and allowed him to lead her into the house.

Veronica appeared at the top of the stairs, her eyes zeroing in on their hands. Georgia instinctively tried to pull away, but Zak held fast. His eyes locked with Veronica's, and it was as if they were communicating. She looked pissed. He looked impassive. She whirled and disappeared from sight, her vamp speed making it impossible for Georgia to follow her movements.

Georgia watched Zak with a frown, confused. After the silent altercation with Veronica, he'd led her into the kitchen, made them both a coffee, and updated her on the progress in the house as if nothing had happened. He was playing with the ring, turning it around and around on his finger, drawing her gaze.

"Does it mean anything?" She gulped, not daring to believe that maybe, just maybe, she might be able to get the ring away from him.

"The ring?" At her nod, he looked down at it and then back at her. "It was my mother's. I'm not overly sentimental, but it's an attractive design, so I wear it."

"Is it valuable? It looks old."

"Its only value is to me. It's made of platinum, so you might get a few dollars if you were to pawn it, but it has no precious gems and no historical value. My mother gave it to my father as a gift; it is all that I have of them, and as I said, I quite like it, so I wear it rather than having it stuffed away in the back of a drawer."

"Yeah, the design is unusual...can I try it on?"

Zak froze. "No."

"I thought you said you weren't sentimental?"

"On most things, I'm not. Why are you so interested?"

Realizing she was close to giving herself away with her fixation on the damn ring, she shrugged casually and took a sip of her coffee.

"I'm not, really. Just making conversation."

She was a terrible liar. Zak watched her as she rinsed her cup in the sink and left it to drain before heading upstairs. A few minutes later, he heard the buzz of some sort of power tool and knew she'd be engrossed in her work for a couple of hours. He'd watched her often, standing in the doorway while she worked, lost in her own world with no idea he was there.

"Frank."

"Sire." Frank appeared immediately.

"Have a couple of the men keep an eye on Georgia's place—I think there is more to these bruises she keeps turning up with than we realize."

"Vamps, you think? Has she been bitten?"

"No. But something's not right. At first, I thought maybe an ex-boyfriend was behind it, but this morning she asked about the ring." He raised his hand and wriggled his fingers.

"Shit. I wish I knew how the fuck these otherworlders found out about it in the first place!" Frank scratched his head, brow furrowed. "First, the demons in Elen Hills were after it, now vamps here —if it's even vamps we're dealing with."

"We would have smelled demons on her if that were the case," Zak assured the head of his security. "And they wouldn't have gone so lightly on her with the beating. See what you can find out. Discreetly. I don't want them to know we're on to them."

He looked down at the ring again. The thin red line woven into the design contained the blood of three angels: a heavenly angel, a fallen angel, and a black angel. It had been forged eons ago; no one knew its actual age, perhaps the age of the earth itself.

The ring had the power to awaken the original vampire, who had been in slumber for over a thousand years. The angels hadn't been able to prevent the creation of the vampire god; some say the brother to God himself, but they'd found a way to slow him down. Fallen angels can't resist the lure of humans, and many a fallen angel had mated with a human and produced offspring. The crossbreeding of a fallen angel and a witch produced the most powerful witch the earth had seen, and it was she who had tricked and lured the vampire God into her web. While she hadn't been able to give him final death, she'd cast a spell on him that sent him into an eternal sleep. There has to be a way to break it and balance the energy with every spell, so the witch created the ring, keeping the energy balanced.

The ring had been passed down throughout Zak's mother's family. When she became fallen and married his father, the Angels agreed she should bring the ring into the mortal realm, believing it would be safer and well hidden. When his parents had been slain, Zak had taken the ring from his dead mother's finger and pushed it onto his own, her blood bathing his skin. He'd felt the magic flare as the ring connected with him and resized to fit him perfectly. The ring was blessed with magic, creating a field around it so that people didn't notice it; no one ever commented or asked him about it. It concerned him greatly that Georgia had asked. She'd noticed it, could see it clearly. He suspected she knew nothing of its origins or power and that someone who did was using her to try and get the ring from him. She probably wasn't aware that the only way the ring could leave his finger was upon his death.

G eorgia was sitting on the floor, a large
piece of wood resting across her lap as
she worked at it slowly with a chisel
and hammer, carving an intricate design into the
wood that would end up as one of the end posts of
the bed.

"I forgot to do something earlier," Zak spoke
from the doorway, causing her to jump. Her senses
were really letting her down when it came to him.
Maybe it was because there were so many vampires
in the house that her senses were on the fritz.

"Oh?" She looked up as he strode across the
room to her, dropping to one knee in front of her
while wrapping a hand around the back of her neck.

Her skin sparked where it touched his, his hand hot against her flesh and getting hotter by the second. Her gaze dropped from his dark eyes to his lips, now so close to her. He was going to kiss her, and heaven help her, she wanted him to. Desire thickened the air around them, her heart thumped against her ribs, and her eyes drifted closed.

Rather than the touch of his lips, she felt the same flare of burning pain followed by the white healing sparkle of his touch as he smoothed away the bruises on her neck and cheek. She opened her eyes in surprise.

"No more freebies."

"Freebies?"

"That's twice now I've healed you, with nothing in return. From now on, there's a price."

"A price?" she squeaked.

"Mmmm. Depending on how injured you are as to what the price is. A bruise can be healed with a kiss. Broken bones require something more."

"I didn't ask you to heal me." She tried to pull back, but his hand was still wrapped around the back of her neck.

"I can't have you wandering around all bruised and broken. That's not how I treat my women."

"I'm not one of your women."

"You will be." He grinned.

"Don't flatter yourself!" she huffed, pushing at his chest. He left without the kiss she'd been longing for.

CHAPTER
TEN

"Try not to be late. Seven sharp," the text said.

"I'll be there," Georgia texted back.

It was Saturday afternoon, and the band Rhys had talked them into seeing was playing at the pub that night. They'd arranged for a group of them to meet at the pub for dinner first.

She'd finished up in her workshop early so she could wash and dry her hair in time for this evening. Being so thick and heavy, it took a while. She'd blasted it with her hairdryer to get most of the moisture out before styling with a curling brush, creating big loose curls that tumbled down her back and around her shoulders. Since it was a bit of a special occasion, Georgia broke out the makeup, accentuating her eyes with a smoky look, lavishing on mascara to create long, dramatic eyelashes. A touch of blush on her cheekbones and a smear of lip gloss finished the look perfectly.

Knowing that her usual jeans and a tank top wouldn't cut it, she settled on a strapless white maxi dress that swirled around her ankles. She pulled the dress in around her waist with a wide tan belt and slipped her feet into matching tan sandals. She slipped on gold hoop earrings and adorned her wrist with matching gold bracelets.

Arriving in a taxi, Georgia made her way to the table Skye had reserved. Her sister and half a dozen friends were already there. After hugs and hellos, Georgia nabbed the empty seat next to Rhys.

"You look amazing," he told her, mouth near her ear due to the noise in the room. The pub was packed; the anticipation in the room was electric.

Georgia looked at Rhys and returned the compliment. In a black shirt, sleeves rolled up to the elbows, and the top buttons were undone so she could see a smattering of chest hair. He was exuding a fair amount of sex appeal himself. His wolf also raised the temperature, seemingly on the alert with so many people in the room.

They ordered drinks and food and caught up on

what everyone had been up to. The band wasn't due to start playing until later in the evening, so the jukebox was getting a fair workout until then. Georgia laughed and drank and relaxed in the company of good friends. Her drinking binges of the last month had been lonely affairs; she'd simply turned up at the pub, planted herself on a stool at the bar, and proceeded to write herself off.

One of the guys returned from the bar with a tray of shots, which were quickly tossed back. Another round of shots, and she was ten foot tall and bullet-proof. Well, actually, she thought she was a disco queen and could sing like Beyonce! The perils of booze.

"Zak's doing a book signing next door tomorrow afternoon." Skye leaned over and spoke loudly in her ear.

"Yeah, so?"

"Perhaps you'd like him to autograph one of your books." Skye teased.

"As if," Georgia scoffed.

"I think you like him," Skye commented. Georgia remained quiet. It bothered her that she did like Zak. Well, she lusted after him anyway, if that counted.

"Zak's here," Skye said suddenly. "Um. He's not alone."

"What?" Georgia leaned forward and followed Skye's line of sight.

Zak stood at the bar, smiling into the eyes of Veronica. The leggy blonde had a hand resting on his chest and was laughing at whatever it was he'd said. Her body turned into his in a familiar, intimate way.

"I thought he told you he wasn't dating her." Skye frowned.

"Yeah. He did. I wasn't sure whether to believe him or not. She's the one who warned me off. He told me she's his PA."

She watched the two of them laughing and talking, heads close together.

"I dunno. Watching them, I'm getting the sense he's not that into her. She's trying really hard to make it look like he is." Skye continued to study them.

"It doesn't matter," Georgia said with a shrug.

"Yeah, it does."

The waitress arrived with another tray filled with drinks. Georgia helped herself to a whiskey, the golden liquid burning a fiery trail down her throat. So much for not needing the anesthetic effects of alcohol tonight.

Doing her best to put all thoughts of Zak out of her mind, Georgia threw herself into having a good time. As soon as the band started, she was up on the dance floor, body moving to the music, letting the rhythm flow through her. She danced until the band took a break, her face flushed and her brow damp.

Pushing her way through the crowd, she leaned against the bar, waiting for the bartender to come back when Zak pressed in behind her. It was standing room only, so she couldn't really tell him off for crowding her, even though she got the feeling it was intentional.

"You're full of surprises tonight," he grinned, a dimple flashing. Before she could stop herself, her hand had reached up, her finger tracking the indentation in his cheek. His smile widened. She realized what she'd done and snatched her hand away.

"Sorry," she muttered, "too much drink."

"I think I like you with too much drink."

"You'd take advantage."

"Damn straight, I would. You look stunning, by the way. As I'm sure every male in the room has told you tonight."

"Errr, no, creepy. But thank you. I think."

The bartender arrived, and because Zak was setting her nerves on edge, she ordered a scotch and coke when she'd meant to order water. She quickly slugged back a mouthful of Dutch courage.

"Why are you here talking to me? Shouldn't you be sweeping Veronica or some other woman off her feet?"

"I'm trying my best, but she's not cooperating," he shrugged. Urgh, the man was infuriating. She pushed past him, ignoring the way her body pressed intimately up against him when he wouldn't move.

"Do you mind?" she sniped.

"Not in the least." His hands settled on her waist to steady her as the crowd surged and pushed her even closer against him. Heat sizzled through her dress where his hands rested, and for a moment, she was tempted to give in and lean against him. The moment passed, and she struggled away, forcing her way through the crowd and back to her table.

ZAK WATCHED as Georgia smiled warmly at Rhys and willingly placed her hand in his. He'd seen a different side to her tonight, one that wasn't all work, fear and holding out on him. And he liked it, liked seeing this carefree side of her.

When he'd watched her move so sensuously on the dance floor, he'd felt himself harden at the sight of her in that dress. It was the first time he'd ever seen her in a dress, and boy, what a sight she was. She'd left her hair loose, and it fell in a tumble of curls and waves down around her shoulders and back. Every now and then, she'd lift the long tresses away from her heated skin and give him a glimpse of her bare shoulders and sleek back.

His interest in her increased tenfold. He was definitely getting her into his bed.

While she stepped into Rhys's arms and swayed with him to the music, Zak sought out Skye, who was only too obliging to accept his offer. He twirled her onto the dance floor, dipping her backward and then pulling her back up into his arms and against his chest. She squealed in delight.

Georgia frowned at him, and he returned her frown with another grin. Two could play this game. Pulling Skye in close, she melted against him, her arms wrapping around his neck, her head resting against his chest. He had the exact same effect on every woman in the room except for Georgia.

The song came to an end, and he stepped back. Skye was reluctant to let him go, but he murmured in her ear, and she soon smiled at him and sashayed away, heading toward Rhys and Georgia, who had remained on the dance floor. Skye claimed Rhys for a dance. He was too much of a gentleman to refuse, a fact Zak was counting on.

"I do believe they're playing our song." He stepped in front of Georgia and pulled her into his embrace, taking her by surprise.

"Bullshit they are," she growled.

"Let's call a truce and enjoy the dance, hmm?" he murmured, slowly easing her closer, brushing his hips against hers and allowing his large hands to skim down her bare back. She shivered in his embrace.

"Okay," she murmured, her surrender catching him by surprise. He must give her alcohol more often.

He swept one hand up beneath the heavy curtain of her hair to rest on the nape of her neck, while the other he kept at the small of her back, enjoying the feel of her pressed up against him. She relaxed against him, one arm sliding around his waist, the other resting on his chest.

The song went on forever but was over all too soon. At least that's what it felt like. He could have stayed in that moment with Georgia, forever. It shook him to realize he felt that way. Women were not creatures he considered entering into a relationship with; he enjoyed them for the mutual pleasure they could bring each other, for the food source they were, and nothing more. And he wasn't used to being told no. Again he cursed that he didn't know what she was thinking, but she seemed as content to be in his arms as he was to have her there.

One song flowed into the next, and still, they swayed to the music. He'd slowly maneuvered them around the dance floor, away from the flashing of mobile phone cameras. He'd have to glamor some of the townsfolk again; their interest in him was ramping up, and he knew from experience that a group of rabid, lust-filled fans ended up being nothing but an annoyance he wasn't in the mood to deal with.

FLOATING ON A CLOUD OF BLISS, Georgia could have stayed in Zak's arms forever; however, the reality was intruding. She needed a bathroom break—all that alcohol was making itself known to her bladder. She lifted her head, moving a fraction of an inch away from him. He immediately tightened his grip, his lips moving to her ear.

"What is it?" His lips touched her ear as he spoke, sending shivers of desire through her. She felt her nipples harden beneath the dress, worried he'd feel her reaction since she was pressed so tightly against him.

"I need a break," she murmured, looking up at him, losing herself in his hot gaze.

"A break?" he frowned, not understanding.

"A toilet break. I need to pee."

He chuckled, "Well then, by all means...it's a shame though, things were just...heating up." His eyes fell to her chest, and she knew he could see her arousal. Embarrassed that her body gave her away, she pulled her hair over her shoulders so the strands covered her breasts. Without another word, she moved away, heading for the Ladies.

The pub was hot, and she felt slightly dizzy, the effects of the alcohol making her clumsy as she bumped into a chair. The next drink was definitely water, she vowed. She'd been maneuvering between abandoned tables and chairs when someone blocked her path. A stunning blonde in a red dress who inexplicably reminded her of Jessica Rabbit. She grinned. Veronica scowled.

"Enjoy your dance?" Veronica hissed. Her hostility took Georgia by surprise. Before she could respond, Veronica continued, "I've already warned you. Zak is mine. Oh, he may play around with a new toy from time to time, but he ALWAYS comes back to me. Without fail. So save yourself the heartache, sweetheart."

"He told me you guys weren't an item." Georgia accused, not sure if she should believe the woman or not.

"Oh, did he? Did he say that it's been only a matter of days since he was in my bed?" Georgia felt the color leave her face, "No?" Veronica taunted, a wicked smile curling her blood-red lips, "I didn't think so. You're a game to him, little girl, a challenge. He'll fuck you and then be bored. He'll be back in my bed, where he belongs, where only I know how to please him."

She felt sick. Afraid she was going to vomit on the floor right there in the pub, she pushed past Veronica and hurried to the ladies', hand over her mouth. Thankfully, most women were up on the dance floor, so there were no queues. Quickly locking herself in a cubicle, she stood for a moment, assessing whether she was going to puke or pee first. The feeling of nausea had passed, so she elected to pee, her mind going over the conversation with Veronica. She wasn't really sure the woman was telling the truth—Skye had a point when she'd observed that it looked like Veronica had a thing for Zak but that perhaps he didn't feel the same way. But then again, maybe that was wishful thinking.

She stood at the sink washing her hands, letting the water flow over her wrists, cooling her heated blood, and sobering her just a little.

The crowd at the bar had thinned a bit. Georgia leaned against the end and sipped at her water, noticing that Veronica had cornered Zak on the dance floor. He held her against him, but in a more traditional waltz pose, one hand resting at her waist, the other cradling her hand in his. She watched as he lowered his head, so Veronica could hear him as he spoke to her. Georgia bristled, watching that dark head bent so close to the blonde, his lips near her ear.

A surge of jealousy fired through her, quickly followed by one of anger. Was he really sleeping with Veronica while trying to get Georgia into bed? She hated to think it might be true, but he was from a different world than her, in more ways than one.

Her anger simmered as she watched and sipped her water. They seemed to be having a fair old chitchat, heads close, taking it in turns to speak into each other's ears. Veronica was now pressed right up against him, and he didn't seem to mind. She wrapped both her arms around his neck and pulled his face down so she could reach his ear. Both of his arms were around her, clasped loosely at her lower back. It looked natural, like they'd danced this way before. That they knew each other's bodies. This wasn't new.

Veronica cast a sly glance in Georgia's direction. Making sure she was watching, she guessed. Bitch. The next time Zak lowered his head to speak, Veronica slid her fingers into his hair and pulled his mouth to hers. He didn't pull away, lingering with his mouth against hers for several moments.

Georgia hadn't expected them to kiss, and she certainly hadn't expected the shot of pain that went through her when they did. She cursed herself, stupid, stupid, stupid, blindly putting the glass of water back on the bar, her eyes filling with tears. She had no claim on him. He was free to do what he liked, but to see him kissing Veronica? It hurt. She hated it and hated even more that she cared.

Suddenly her wobbly world was spinning. Horrified that she was about to start howling at the bar like a lovesick teenager, she quickly pushed her way to the exit, keeping her face down so no one could see the tears about to spill. She *never* cried.

Skye appeared at her side, slinging an arm around her waist as Georgia weaved across the floor.

"I gotcha," she grunted. Georgia's drunken mind had trouble processing what she'd seen. All she knew was the pain radiating through her. That and the fact she wanted to punch Veronica right in the face. And Zak. The bastard.

"She's such a fucking bitch," Georgia cursed, focusing on putting one foot in front of the other.

"Can you walk?"

Georgia nodded but wasn't entirely sure. Skye kept one arm around her and navigated them towards the door. They made it outside, and Skye directed them to the alley at the side of the pub. Leaning back against the building, she tilted her face up to the moonlit sky, dragging in gulps of air. Her chest hurt, and her eyes burnt; she felt bruised inside. She didn't want to admit, even to herself, that she was starting to fall for Zak, that she'd been dreaming of him, that she'd started to wonder if perhaps it wouldn't be so bad to give in and sleep with him. But the pain of his betrayal, if you could even call it that, was so intense, so overwhelming, she was at a loss.

Rhys rounded the side of the building.

"Are you ok? I saw you leave. You seemed upset." He strolled down the alley to where she stood, stopping a couple of feet away. He kept his hands in his trouser pockets, eyes darting from Skye to Georgia and back again.

"I'm fine," she sniffed, "just being stupid." She wanted to cry even harder.

"Come on, Georgia. Focus. Let's not cry," Skye soothed her, knowing how much her sister hated to cry.

"I'm focusing," Georgia repeated.

"I need to get her home." Skye looked at Rhys, and he nodded.

"You get your car; I'll wait with her." They exchanged places, Rhys sliding an arm around her and pulling her against his chest. They listened to the sound of Skye's heels clicking against the pavement and then fading into the distance.

A pulse of energy surrounded them. Georgia looked up with blurry eyes. Zak stood three feet away.

"What happened?" he demanded, seeing her tear-stained face, and frowning at her standing in another man's arms.

"Go away," she told him, sniffing. She pushed

away from Rhys, not wanting him drawn into this mess. It was so unfair to him; she shouldn't have let him comfort her. She really was a horrible person.

Both men looked puzzled, unsure who she was telling to go away. Perhaps both. Zak grabbed her hand, but she snatched it back, turning on him with a snarl. "Will you just fuck off!" she yelled, her emotions so strung out she felt she could burst into flames. Pain and anger warred through her, and whenever she glanced at Rhys, guilt too. She hated this. Hated it.

"You saw." Zak nodded with a sigh.

"Everyone fucking saw, Zak—you kissing your girlfriend. You're one twisted bastard, you know that," she cried.

"She's not my girlfriend. I've told you that."

"Your fuckbuddy then? 'Cos, I know you had sex with her just a few days ago, and don't even think of trying to deny it, you asshole," she challenged.

"I'll errr... wait for Skye out the front," Rhys muttered, spinning on his heel and quickly striding away.

Zak crowded her up against the wall with superhuman speed, his body pressed against hers from knee to shoulder.

"Get the fuck off!" she screeched at him,

pushing, and trying to kick, though he had her legs trapped. He grabbed both her wrists and pinned them on either side of her head against the wall. She was trapped. Her heart was thundering in her chest, the pain temporarily forgotten, anger the ruling emotion.

"Calm down," he cursed, her wriggling distracting him until all he wanted to do was rip her clothes off and take her against the wall, here and now. She felt his erection pressed against her stomach and stilled.

"That's better." He lowered his head to press his lips against her neck, softly trailing his tongue over her skin.

"Don't. I'm fucking pissed off with you. You don't get the right to touch me," she growled.

"I know you are." His lips were doing magical things to her neck, things that were making her knees go weak and heat pool between her legs. Damn him.

"You know what I am, yes?" She nodded. "While I am only half-vampire, I still need blood to sustain me. Often, with vampires, sex and blood are not mutually exclusive. Drinking your lover's blood while having sex heightens the experience for both parties."

She was trying to listen, not sure what his words had to do with kissing Veronica, but talk of sex was heightening her arousal.

"I don't understand." With her mind fogged by all she'd had to drink, she couldn't fathom why he was telling her this.

"I have fed from Veronica, and when I've fed, yes, I've fucked her. I sired her 200 years ago; it is inevitable that we would find ourselves in bed together over that period of time. But we are not a romantic item. Our bond is different, and I do not think of her in those terms, although I am starting to see that perhaps I have misjudged her feelings for me."

"So you have sex with her so you can drink her blood."

"Not always. I can drink blood without having sex." He knew where she was headed and wanted to reassure her he wasn't some crazed sex addict. "And Veronica isn't on hand to be my food source—it was the first time in ten years that I'd fed from her, and, by the way, we did not have sex then. No matter what she may have told you."

"Ten years?"

"Yes. She's messing with you, Georgia." He could feel her resistance starting to melt. "She knows I'm interested in you, and she's jealous. I will deal with her; you have nothing to worry about."

"I don't?" she repeated, dazed. His lips were moving up her neck, across her cheek, and he was dropping light caresses against her lips, not deepening it into a kiss, not yet, just teasing her and keeping her on edge. He released her hands to wipe away the wet tears on her cheeks, smiling when she didn't fight him but let her arms rest against his chest.

"It's been a long time since I've had to reassure a woman my interest in her is genuine," he admitted ruefully, resting his forehead against hers, "and it is so much more difficult with you because I can't read what you're thinking...although..." he pondered, lifting his head to look at her.

"What?" she breathed; eyes focused on his mouth—all she could think about was him kissing her.

"Let me taste you." He teased her mouth with his again, this time letting the kiss deepen, invading her mouth with his tongue, stroking and teasing. She wrapped her arms around his neck and pulled herself into his body, her hips thrusting against him. She was lost in a fog of desire, her body felt on fire, and the world was starting to spin.

"Say yes," he said into her mouth.

"Yes." She groaned, head falling back as his hand caressed her breast, and his mouth traveled back to her neck, where he stroked her with that magic tongue. His fingers teased her nipple, and all she could think about was having his hot mouth replace his fingers to have that magic tongue of his teasing her sensitive flesh.

A sharp sting in the side of her neck made her gasp, but then the molten lava that flowed through her veins brought her to her knees. Unable to stand, he supported her against him, pushing the top half of her body against the wall and pulling her legs up around his waist, opening her to him fully. Her dress was hiked up around her waist, and she didn't care. She wanted him. Inside her. Now.

Zak lifted his mouth from her neck, capturing hers in another deep kiss. She tasted the tang of blood on his tongue and knew it was hers but couldn't bring herself to care. With one hand, he reached between them, allowing his fingers to brush against her core. She gasped and jumped at the contact; her nerve endings fried. Instinctively she pushed against his fingers that were now stroking her through her panties; she clutched at his shoulders, pulling him closer to her and trying to move against him but finding it impossible pinned to the wall.

His thumb pressed against her, and she groaned, wanting more, so much more. His fingers brushed, teased, and rubbed as his tongue did wonderful things to her mouth. She could feel the tension building, release so close. His mouth was at her neck again, open and pressed against her hot flesh. This time she knew the sharp sting was his fangs, but the sensation that followed simply melted her mind. As his fangs penetrated her flesh, his thumb pressed in tight circles against her, and she came, exploding like fireworks in his arms, trembling and shivering at the overwhelming sensations flowing throughout her body.

He held her, allowing her legs to slide down to the ground. She watched in a daze as he gently smoothed her dress back into place, then touched a hand to the side of her neck where she felt the familiar tingle of him healing her.

"Ok?" he asked, taking her hand. Speechless, she nodded.

Zak smiled at the dazed woman in front of him. Her cheeks were flushed, and her eyes glazed. She swayed before him, and he pulled her against his chest again, allowing her to rest against him while she gathered herself.

His own arousal was uncomfortably tight in his trousers, with little room for movement, but tonight hadn't been about him. It had been about Georgia. She was probably going to be mad at him when she sobered up and relived the night's events—which is why he didn't have sex with her as badly as he wanted to. Even though he'd told her he'd take advantage of a drunken woman, he wanted Georgia fully alert when they slept together.

He'd hoped that drinking her blood would give him an insight into her mind, and it had to some extent, but her blood was tainted with alcohol, and all that he saw had been blurred, rambling images. He'd felt her emotions, though, the heady passion, the arousing anger, and the cutting pain. He could handle the anger and passion any day; the pain wasn't something he liked to think he was responsible for, but he knew that wasn't the case. Among the blurry images, he'd seen one clear picture. Veronica kissing him. It had hurt Georgia, and for that, he was sorry.

She let out a soft sigh against him, and he looked down at her, her eyes starting to droop.

"Ready for home?" he murmured. She nodded.

Gathering her closer in his arms, he used his magic to teleport them back to her house. Reeling slightly from the sensation of whizzing through time and space, Zak held her tightly until she oriented herself and handed him her front door key. Unlocking the door, he carried her upstairs and into her bedroom. He badly wanted to throw her down on the bed and sink into her, losing himself in her, but she was almost asleep on her feet.

With great restraint, he unclasped her belt and tugged her dress down, leaving her standing before him in a strapless bra and knickers.

"So beautiful," he breathed. She watched him with hooded eyes.

"Are you going to fuck me now?" she wanted to know.

"No," he growled. He pulled the bedcovers back and gently tucked her into bed, pulling the covers up to her neck to hide the temptation of her body.

"Oh." She seemed disappointed, and he chuckled.

"But I will. Soon. I want you to be wide awake and sober when I fuck you. I want you to know exactly what I'm doing, what my touch does to you, what your touch does to me," he told her.

"Ok." She closed her eyes on a sigh, sleep quickly claiming her.

Zak watched her sleep for a moment, brushing her hair away from her forehead and placing an affectionate kiss upon her creamy skin.

Now he had to go and sort Veronica out. What on earth had she been playing at? It wasn't like Veronica to play such games.

CHAPTER
ELEVEN

Georgia woke with a pounding headache and her picture all over social media. A shot of her dancing with Zak, him dipping her back and kissing her neck. Then the images of Veronica in his arms and their kiss. All sorts of speculation on a love triangle dominated the Redmeadows Tribune's Facebook page.

Sitting at her kitchen table nursing a coffee, she slowly sipped as she flicked through her text messages—and there were plenty. Half a dozen from her sister, wanting to make sure she was okay. She'd returned with the car to discover her gone. Thankfully Rhys had told her Zak had taken care of her. A couple from Rhys asking if she was okay. And a ton of sleazy propositions.

She responded to Skye and Rhys, telling them not to believe everything they see and hear, that she was fine but hung-over and wasn't up for company. Which was true. She really didn't have the patience to deal with the idiots of this world today.

A hot shower and a couple of painkillers worked wonders. Loosely braiding her wet hair, she pulled on shorts and a halter neck top when a text arrived from Zak.

"*Come to the book signing*," it read.

"*No.*"

"*We need to talk.*"

"*We truly don't.*"

Turning off her phone, she strolled outside. It was hot. But she loved the heat, loved summer. One day she promised herself a swimming pool. Not yet, though. Now she needed to work hard and save to afford such luxuries. She headed to the workshop; working always soothed her, and right now, her nerve endings were feeling a tad raw. She didn't want to think of Zak... and Veronica... and Zak kissing Veronica... and then Zak kissing and touching her and the other bone-meltingly beautiful things he'd done. No, she didn't want to think, or remember them, at all. *Much*.

Grabbing some sandpaper, she sat on the floor, a

leg on either side of one of the dining table legs, and started sanding. The legs were beautifully curved and had a subtle design, similar to ivy climbing up a terrace, carved into them. She didn't want to obliterate the carvings, which she would have done if she'd used an electric sander. Instead, she painstakingly sanded by hand, bringing the legs, one at a time, back to their natural timber.

The light outside had started to fade when she sat back with a groan, finally finished. Scrambling to her feet, she stretched, easing the kinks out of her protesting muscles and stamping her feet to try and get some feeling back into her backside, which was numb from sitting on the floor for hours on end.

Her senses fired a warning. A vamp was in the vicinity. She wished her early warning system would kick in earlier, giving her time to actually do something to protect herself, but alas, one second she sensed them, the next they were there.

This time she had two visitors. She recognized the thug vamp, but not the taller, slimmer one moving ahead of him. Power rolled off him in waves.

"You, Georgia Pearce, have created quite a stir amongst my people." The tall blonde vamp spoke. "Allow me to introduce myself. I'm Erik."

"I suppose good manners dictate I say I'm

pleased to meet you, but I'm not. What do you want?"

"You're right," Erik smiled, turning to the thug vamp behind him, "she is feisty."

"Told you."

"I had to see for myself this human female who broke a vampire's nose," Erik said, moving around her and studying her intently from every angle. She froze.

"However, no matter how intriguing I find you, or how feisty you may be, the fact still remains that you have not done what was requested of you, Georgia." He tsked like she was a naughty child.

"Nothing has been 'requested' of me," she snapped, "your thug comes in here, threatens me, hurts me, and you expect me to go and steal some guy's jewelry?"

"The ring will be mine, Georgia, and *you will* retrieve it for me. I can see that you're strong-willed, so I'm going to give you two more days to get the ring—with a little extra persuasion, I know you can do it." He smiled slightly, running a finger down her cheek.

"You smell delicious, by the way," he murmured, eyes dropping to her chest before rising up to settle on her lips, then meeting her eyes once more. "Next time we meet, I shall have you... unless you have the ring."

And then he was gone.

Heart thumping in her chest, she dragged a deep breath into her burning lungs, not realizing she'd been holding it while Erik had been sizing her up as his next meal. She wasn't sure if he intended to bite her or rape her or both.

SHE SOAKED IN A HOT BATH, easing away the aches in her muscles but not the worry from her mind. She didn't know how on earth she was going to get out of this mess. She'd been thinking about telling Zak until he'd kissed Veronica right in front of her. She couldn't trust him. That much was clear. He'd lied through his teeth about the other woman. She didn't want to think about what he'd done to her in the alley. The way he'd touched her made her fall apart in his arms.

She vaguely remembered him bringing her home; she thought she'd tried to initiate sex with him, but he'd said no. Her memories were fuzzy, and she couldn't really be sure what had happened. Still, she'd woken up this morning wearing nothing but her underwear. Why hadn't he stayed if he wanted her as badly as he said he did? What game was he playing?

She was curled up on the sofa mindlessly watching TV when her mobile rang. It was Rhys, and she was tempted to ignore it, feeling bad.

"Hi," she finally answered, muting the TV.

"You'd better get down here," Rhys's voice sounded stressed, "your shop is on fire."

"What?" She shot to her feet, already heading towards the front door, scooping her keys off the coffee table as she went.

"Just get here." Rhys hung up.

She sped all the way into town, trying to dial Skye and keep her attention on the road. Skye didn't answer. *Please let her be okay*, Georgia prayed.

Fire trucks were in the street out front of the shop, and a group of spectators had gathered. Georgia ran up, screaming Skye's name. Strong arms grabbed her from behind, stopping her from rushing into the burning building. Georgia struggled against Rhys's hold, terrified her sister was inside, dying.

"Let me go!" She swore, stomping on Rhys's foot and getting ready to elbow him in the stomach.

"She's ok! Skye is ok! She's not in there." Rhys

shouted in her ear. She stilled, and he slowly released his hold on her.

"She's at a friend's place, has been all afternoon. She's safe."

A tear ran down Georgia's cheek, the relief overwhelming. She sank to her knees on the sidewalk, trying not to hyperventilate, but judging by the dizzy feeling, she wasn't succeeding.

"How did this happen?" she croaked.

"Not sure until we get the fire out and can investigate," the fire chief told her. Rhys gave her a hand up and kept a steadying hand on her shoulder.

She had nothing to say. No words. The shop was their livelihood. Had been their life since the death of their parents, and they'd poured their hearts and souls into the place. And now it was gone, reduced to a pile of soggy ashes. She couldn't comprehend it.

Hours passed, and Georgia stood on the sidewalk, looking at the burnt-out shop. Police tape now covered the front, keeping people away. Skye had arrived, cried in her arms, and had been taken away by Rhys. The crowd left, the excitement over. The street was quiet, the smell of smoke heavy in the air. It must have been after midnight, yet Georgia stayed. Everyone had tried to persuade her to leave, but she couldn't. So she waited. Finally, she felt it, the zap in her senses that told her a vampire was nearby.

"Was this you?" she asked Erik as he stood beside her and surveyed the burnt-out building.

"You needed incentive."

She turned to look at him. "What if my sister had been home? Her flat is just above the shop. She could have died!"

He shrugged, "Whatever it takes. You will do as I ask, Georgia or those around you will pay. Do I make myself clear?" His voice was cold, void of all emotion. She nodded. He stared into her eyes for a moment before suddenly turning his head as if listening. Something had caught his attention. Then he was gone. Georgia couldn't tell if he teleported or simply moved at a vampiric speed.

Moments later, Zak appeared in front of her. He looked at the burnt-out mess that had once been her shop, then at her.

He opened his mouth to say something but must've thought better of it, 'cos he shut it again without speaking.

S he was a vision before him, her hair wild and loose, tumbling to her waist. She stood in track pants, a t-shirt, and no shoes, a smudge of soot across her cheek, yet still, she was the most beautiful woman he'd ever seen. Her eyes looked bruised, the pain in them deep, but there was also something else. Fear.

He moved toward her, about to demand that she tell him what the fuck was going on, when a scent stopped him short. Over the stench of smoke, he could smell vampire. Not one of his, someone different. He shut his mouth without saying a word.

"Come on." He pulled her into his arms and teleported them back to her place before she could protest.

The place was a mess and reeked of vampires. Furniture was tipped over, drawers opened, and their contents tipped out.

"Mother fucker!" Georgia cursed, hands-on-hips as she surveyed the damage. Zak quickly scanned the house; every room had been trashed.

"Looks like you're in some serious shit," he commented, coming back to her side and holding out a hand to her. She arched a brow. "Come on. You can't stay here." He watched her wrestle with the idea of going with him, but common sense won out, and she placed a hand in his. He pulled her into his chest, wrapped his other arm around her, and teleported them back to his place.

He could feel the angry energy from her, thankful that it had pulled her out of the shock that he'd found her in. He sank into the plush sofa and watched as she paced back and forth in his lounge room, muttering and cursing under her breath.

"So," he inquired casually as if having your shop burnt down and your house ransacked was an everyday occurrence, "ready to tell me what the fuck is going on?"

She plopped down on the sofa at the opposite end, then quickly rose to begin pacing again. She'd stop, look at him, consider, then start pacing again. He felt tired watching her.

"Where's Veronica?" she suddenly asked.

"Gone back to Elen Hills for a while," he shrugged like it was no big deal. He'd sent her back; she clearly needed some space from him. He'd read her when he'd kissed her the night before, the kiss simply a means to gain access to what she'd previously hidden in her mind. He'd been stunned by what he'd found. Veronica was insanely jealous of Georgia, believed that he and Veronica were destined to be life mates, and was prepared to take out the competition. They'd also been a hidden corner in her mind, a wall she'd put up that he hadn't been able to get around, which worried him. She was hiding something big. Until he found out what it was, he'd sent her to the other side of the world. She had been seething angry at him but unable to disobey a direct command from her sire.

Georgia didn't comment but seemed to be mulling that over. She sat in an armchair and curled her legs up beneath her.

"I'm usually a fairly patient man, but for some reason, with you..." he let his voice trail off.

"I bring out the best in people." She shrugged. Moving so fast she couldn't see, he knelt on the floor in front of her chair, his hands resting on the armrests on either side of her, effectively trapping her.

"You tempt me beyond reason," he murmured, closing in on her. He could hear her heart thumping in her chest and knew she was just as affected as he was. Cupping her cheeks in his palms, he forced her eyes to meet his.

"Say yes."

A memory triggered from last night, when he'd said those exact words and when she'd said those words, how her world had exploded in bliss. Did she want that again? Hell yes.

"Yes," she whispered, for once compliant.

His lips crushed hers, trying to be gentle but desperate for a taste. She opened beneath him, allowing access, her tongue dueling with his. He pulled her closer, pulling her legs so that they were no longer beneath her but wrapped around his waist. With a tug, her t-shirt was gone. He cupped a breast, and she groaned into his mouth, pushing herself into his palm. Another flick, and her bra was gone, leaving her breasts bare. The feel of her hot skin in his hand was electrifying. He dragged his mouth from hers, trailing hot kisses down her neck and across her chest until he reached his goal.

Pulling a nipple into his mouth, he nuzzled, sucked, and nipped while she whimpered and moaned against him.

He allowed his fangs to descend, scraping them gently across her sensitive flesh, moving his attention from one breast to the other. She ran her fingers through his hair, pulling his head to her chest.

She jumped a little at the tearing of fabric as he literally ripped her track pants and panties away, leaving her naked to his gaze and touch. As he continued his assault on her breasts, he let his fingers trail down her stomach, her thighs before slowly skipping across her skin to the core of her. He parted her folds; she was so hot and wet for him. His cock was rock hard in his jeans, but he held back from plunging into her. He pushed his fingers into her, and she clasped him tightly, a loud groan escaping from her throat. He moved his mouth back up to hers, kissing her again, devouring her with his lips and tongue as his fingers moved within her.

"Now." She gasped, arching her hips and pushing against his hand.

"Not yet, sweetheart," he chuckled. He'd waited this long for her; he was going to enjoy every moment. Disentangling himself from her grasp, he unwrapped her legs from his waist and pushed her back until she was almost flat against the cushion of the chair, her hips held firm in his grasp. His eyes took her in, her full breasts with dusky colored nipples, her smooth skin, flat stomach, and then the heaven between her thighs, spread before him in invitation.

He dropped his head to her with a groan, stroking along her center with his tongue. She twitched at the sensations and went to grab his head, but he held her hands captive. Oh, he wasn't done tasting her yet. He alternated between thrusting his tongue into her and laving her. He could feel her tense beneath him, her breath catching in her throat as her orgasm approached. He released one hand to push two fingers deep into her while his tongue continued to lap at her. She was so, so close. Her whole body was bowed and tense beneath him. With a fang, he gently pierced her delicate skin, and she screamed, her orgasm bursting over her. He plunged his tongue into her, tasting her as she flooded over him, her legs shaking.

Wasting no time, he freed himself from his jeans and plunged into her. She arched at the hardness of him, trying to rise to wrap herself around him, but he held her flat with a palm on her stomach.

"Look at me," he growled. He looked into her eyes as he slowly withdrew so only the tip of his cock was in her, then slid slowly back in, all the way. Her breath caught in her throat, and her eyes started to close.

"No." He rammed into her hard, and her eyes sprang open. "Look at me," he commanded again. This time she kept her eyes on his as he alternated between slow and smooth and hard and fast.

She struggled to sit up again, and he realized she was getting uncomfortable in the position he had her in. With a flip, he had them both stretched out on the sofa, still pushing into her relentlessly without missing a beat. She lay beneath him, legs wrapped around him and pushing her hips up to meet each thrust. Her hand pulled his shirt over his head, and he only then realized she was the only one naked; his pants were around his thighs, the only part of him that needed to be naked was buried in her sweet flesh.

He groaned against her when she ran her hands up and down his back, enjoying the feel of him as much as he was enjoying her.

"Harder," she whispered, dropping kisses

against his neck. He obliged, slamming into her as deep as he could go, and she welcomed every thrust, her body rising to meet his as if she couldn't get enough of him. He used vampiric speed thrusts for a second, sliding in and out of her so fast the sensations were overwhelming.

He could feel the beginning of his own orgasm and slowed the pace back to human speed again. She was groaning and whimpering in his arms, her head thrown back as she balanced on the edge of another orgasm. Her long neck beckoned him, and with his hips thrusting into her, he lowered his mouth and bit, sucking the nectar of her blood down his throat.

His orgasm roared through him, and she cried aloud beneath him, her internal muscles clenched around his cock so hard it was heaven. Two more hard thrusts, and he shot into her while his mind battled all the images assaulting his brain from drinking her blood. It was as he'd suspected, drinking from her opened her mind to him, but in the middle of fucking it was too difficult to concentrate on what he'd seen; she totally filled him with sensation, her blood the sweetest wine in his mouth while her muscles contracted just as sweetly around him.

Warm, cozy, and unbelievably sated, Georgia snuggled beneath the covers, her eyes slowly blinking open. Only she wasn't in her bed or her room. Memories of last night returned; after the unbelievable session in the lounge room, they'd moved to Zak's bedroom and spent a very long night exploring and satisfying each other. Oh, my god, this man had moves; he knew exactly where to touch, how much pressure to apply, how to keep her on edge and then push her over into mind-blowing orgasms.

A peek over her shoulder revealed Zak sprawled out next to her, sound asleep. Slowly she wriggled out of bed and silently crept across the room, keen to get out of there without waking him up. As much as last night had been the best sex of her life, she'd done what she'd told herself she wouldn't do. Slept with Zak Goodwin. And now she was another notch on that infamous bedpost of his. Damn it.

Needing space and needing to sort out the mess her life had become, she quickly darted downstairs to the lounge room, praying to God no one was around to see her naked ass running around the house while she quickly gathered up her clothes.

Her track pants and knickers were ruined; thankfully, her t-shirt was long enough to just cover her. She looked around for her keys when it hit her —he'd teleported her here. She had no transport, no keys, no phone; she didn't even have shoes. Fuck!

Ordinarily, a ten-mile walk wouldn't faze her, but with no shoes? No thanks. She turned and headed toward the kitchen; maybe she could find someone to give her a lift. Someone who wouldn't wake Zak up first and tell him she was leaving. But then, perhaps this is how things usually played out when he had an overnight guest. He slept in while the staff got rid of the woman. Imagination going into overdrive, she almost walked into Frank.

"Frank!" she exclaimed, for once pleased to see the brute of a man.

"Georgia." He looked her up and down, undoubtedly knowing she was naked beneath the t-shirt. "New work attire?" he teased, mouth curling up in a grin.

"Har, har," she snapped, realizing she looked like she'd just crawled out of bed, with her hair tousled around her and hanging loose and a distinct lack of clothing and footwear. "I need a lift. Now. Can you drop me in town?"

"Sure." He ushered her ahead of him back

towards the front of the house. She liked that he didn't question or comment on what had obviously gone down between her and Zak.

Frank pulled in next to her truck, engine idling while she jumped out and checked that her keys were where she'd left them... in the ignition. Climbing behind the wheel, she gunned the engine and headed for home. As she pulled up in the driveway, she felt with her senses, testing the boundaries to see if she had any supernatural visitors. Thankfully she felt nothing and proceeded into the house—it was going to be a long day cleaning up the mess. And then there was the shop to deal with.

First, a quick shower to wash away the faint scent of smoke and the stronger scent of Zak. No doubt Frank had smelt him all over her, which annoyed her. Georgia liked her business to remain her business. She hadn't even had the chance to really think about how she felt about Zak and didn't particularly want it public knowledge that she was sleeping with the guy. Well, slept with the guy. Who knew if there'd be a repeat performance?

She spent all morning straightening up the house, and that was just downstairs. She hadn't even started upstairs yet. Her body ached, partly from last night's activities and partly from lifting and moving furniture. She hadn't heard from Zak.

Taking a break, she pulled out her phone and speed-dialed her sister.

"Hey, Skye—you okay?"

"Yeah. Really bummed about the shop. Can you believe it? Rhys said we can't go in until we've got the all-clear from the inspectors that the building is safe."

"Hopefully, they're quick about it, and we can get into your apartment and at least get some clothes for you."

"Agreed. I'm still wearing yesterday's clothes— okay if I come out and raid your wardrobe?"

"Of course. You're staying with me until this gets sorted anyway—you know your room here is always waiting."

"Thanks, sis. I'll let Cindy know I'm leaving, should be there in twenty."

After hanging up with her sister, she rang Rhys, who told her what Skye had already said. No access until the building was declared safe. The apartment wasn't damaged by fire but had sustained some smoke and water damage. The shop was pretty gutted, and the inspectors needed to make sure it was structurally sound before they'd let anyone back in. Initial reports indicated the fire had been deliberately lit. What a surprise.

Georgia had just enough time to straighten up the spare room and close the door on her own trashed bedroom before Skye arrived.

They spent the afternoon on the back porch, Skye on the phone with the insurance company and making lists of everything they needed to do, while Georgia continued with the carvings for Zak's bedroom suite. The headboard was finished; she just needed to complete the footboard, and the bed would be ready to assemble. She listened as her ever-efficient sister handled the shop's temporary, hopefully, closure and discussed ideas for storage of any pieces that weren't totally ruined by the fire or water—which they wouldn't know until they could get in and see for themselves.

An approaching car had the sisters looking at each other before a *toot* reached their ears. Skye leaped to her feet, "That's probably Rhys," scrambling inside to greet their visitor. Georgia continued with her carving, running her fingers over the intricate design, pleased with how it had turned out.

"Hey, how are you today." Rhys followed Skye

back out onto the deck, a six-pack of beers in one hand, pizza in the other.

"I'm good. Sorry for wigging out on you last night." Georgia admitted sheepishly.

"Hey, I'd be pretty freaked if I'd thought either of you was in that fire. Don't worry about it. The main thing is you're both safe."

He plopped down into a chair and passed out the beers before opening the pizza box and offering them a slice. Georgia accepted both, putting her carving aside and brushing off all the wood shavings. She hadn't realized how hungry she was until he'd opened the pizza box, and the delicious smells had wafted her way.

"Well ladies, the good news is you can return to your shop." As both girls made a move to rise, he shushed them back, "Not tonight! Tomorrow, you can return tomorrow. Your apartment is okay, Skye, structurally, that is. No water damage but lots of smoke and soot. The shop is also structurally okay, but it's been gutted—doubtful you can salvage any of your stock, but I'll leave that to you to determine. You'll now need wiring, repairs to the floor where the fire started, plus of course, new flooring and painting—you're insured, right?"

"Of course," Skye scoffed, "I've already been in

touch with our agent, and he's emailing me claim forms today—they need to send their own assessor before we do any repairs, so hopefully, I can get that organized quickly while we get quotes for the repairs. Actually, I'm going to check if he's sent them yet." She scrambled to her feet and carried her pizza and beer inside.

"Actually, I'm glad I got you alone," Rhys leaned toward Georgia, his face earnest.

"Oh?"

"Your place...this place here, the farm...it stinks of vampire. Did something happen?" She hadn't considered that his werewolf nose would have picked up on the scents of the vampires and couldn't hide the surprise that flashed across her face.

"Nothing for you to worry about, Rhys," she assured him. The less involved he was, the better; the last thing she needed was for him to be at risk because of her as well.

"Jesus, Georgia," he exploded, shoving his pizza aside and grabbing her wrist, "I know something's going on. I'm not fucking stupid. I'm a bloody cop, for God's sake, not only have I been trained to spot this type of shit, but my wolf isn't stupid either!"

She jerked back from his sudden attack, feeling bad for lying to her best friend.

"Rhys!" He yanked hard on her wrist, making her lose her balance and fall against his chest, where he held her hard against him.

"I'm fucking worried about you, ok? I got a whiff of a vampire at the shop last night, this place reeks of vampires, and I'm pretty sure I can smell something on you." He pushed his nose into her neck and took a deep breath in through his nose, smelling her. He raised his head slightly, frowning at her, then pressed his face against her neck again and took another sniff, "What is that?" he murmured.

"*That* would be me."

Georgia jerked out of Rhys's hold at the sound of Zak's voice. *Oh great.*

"I didn't hear you pull up." Rhys frowned at Zak, where he stood leaning against the bottom step of the deck.

"Could be because you were too distracted putting your nose on my woman," Zak drawled, ignoring Georgia's outraged hiss as he casually made his way up the stairs towards them.

"Your woman? Is that what I can smell on you? Him?" Rhys turned an accusing glare her way. *Oh fuck.* Even though Rhys knew she didn't feel for him that way, she still didn't intentionally want to hurt him.

"Rhys—" she began, only to have Zak cut her off. "Yeah, that's probably me you can smell on her. We were all over each other last night."

Rhys's face darkened in anger. He glared at her. "You spent the night with him?" *Oh, what the hell.* She nodded, locking eyes with Zak so he could see how pissed off she was.

"Fuck," Rhys swore, shoving to his feet and stalking away.

"Exactly." Zak agreed, earning himself a swift kick from Georgia.

Skye chose that moment to come back outside, noticing the thick tension in the air.

"Oh hi," she threw a smile at Zak, then looked at Rhys with a frown. "Everything okay?"

"Oh, everything's just fine if you think your sister slutting around with him is okay!" Rhys growled.

Georgia sucked in a hurt breath at his words. Before either of the girls could say anything, Zak had Rhys up against the back of the house with his hand wrapped around his throat,

"You NEVER speak that way about her again, you understand?" His anger was like an invisible force surrounding them all. "You have no claims on her, pup, and if you can't control your jealousy, then I suggest you stay away. Far away."

The silence that followed was thick and heavy while the werewolf and vamp-angel squared off. Finally, Rhys nodded abruptly. Zak dropped his hand and moved back to Georgia's side, sliding a proprietary arm around her waist and drawing her into his side. Skye watched with wide eyes before blowing out a breath and dropping into a seat. "Well, there you go." She tipped her beer bottle at Georgia and Zak in salute before taking a long swallow.

Rhys left without a word. Georgia's heart ached, knowing their relationship had irrevocably changed. She just hoped she hadn't lost her friend forever. Feeling sad, she leaned into Zak and dropped her head against his shoulder for a moment, gathering her thoughts. The arm around her waist tightened in response, and she felt him drop a kiss on the top of her head.

"So what did you two lovely ladies get up to today?" he inquired, helping himself to a beer and slice of pizza, and plopping himself down into the seat that Rhys had occupied. Georgia settled back into her own chair and resumed eating while Skye happily babbled away about what was happening with the shop.

"So. You two." She indicated the pair of them. "An item?"

"Yes," Zak answered, arching a brow at Georgia when she instinctively shook her head.

"Good," Skye declared, "it's about time she had some fun. Just don't hurt her," she warned him.

"Never," he assured her.

"Well then, I'll give the pair of you some space. I'll be in my room. Listening to music. With my headphones on." She grinned cheekily before scooping up more pizza and heading back into the house.

THIRTEEN

Z ak knew Georgia was sitting there wallowing in guilt over Rhys. Last night had given him more than mind-blowing sex. It had given him her mind, a virtual open book. She had no walls, nothing hidden away. At the time, he'd been enjoying their activities too much to delve, but after she'd snuck out this morning, he lay in bed and carefully combed through her mind. Even though they were no longer connected, it was like he'd downloaded all her memories and was able to retrieve them one at a time.

He knew she was freaked out about sleeping with him; he didn't have to read her mind to learn that, so he'd let her have her space while he studied her life. He knew she'd be royally pissed if she knew what he'd done, which is why he had no intention of telling her.

"He'll be fine," he told her now, knowing she was fretting and worrying about her friend, who was in pain.

"How do you know," she grumbled at him.

"Because he only thinks he's in love with you. Like you, he loves you like a sister. He just doesn't realize it yet. Plus, he's a werewolf—when he meets his true mate, he'll know that what he feels for you is nothing compared to the emotion of connecting with his mate."

"Did you read his mind?" she bristled.

"Not tonight. But you have to remember, Georgia, I've been around a long time."

"You've seen it all before?" she drawled.

"Exactly. You beat yourself up over this, but you've done nothing to lead him on, yet you feel selfish because you value his friendship too much to push him out of your life."

She nodded, looking off into the distance. The sun had set, and the stars were starting to come out. She loved this time of evening. Even better to be sitting outside, drinking beer and eating pizza. Then she'd remember that it was Rhys who had provided both and felt sad again.

"I take it those two don't know about what happened here last night?" Zak indicated the house.

"No. I got most of it cleaned up. Just need to get my room sorted. I don't want to scare Skye and Rhys... well, it would just make a bad situation worse. He'd probably want to camp on the sofa or something to keep us safe, and I'm not sure that's such a good idea."

"It's definitely not a good idea," Zak agreed. He pulled the cushion off the chair next to him and placed it on the deck between his feet. "Come here. You're tense. Let me help."

She moved to the cushion, sitting cross-legged between his legs. He brushed her hair forward over her shoulder before slowly massaging her neck and shoulders. His firm touch was pure bliss, and she groaned as he worked on the knots.

She lost track of time as his hands soothed her, her chin practically resting on her chest. She felt warm and lethargic and soooo relaxed. And for that moment in time, there was nowhere in the world she'd rather be. That thought alone should have scared the pants off her, yet strangely it didn't. When she was with Zak, it felt right. It was only when she remembered the hundreds of women who'd been before her that he'd done this with, who he'd touched like he'd touched her, that she doubted her sanity in getting involved with this man. He was worming his way into her life, a life she rarely shared with others. She had no doubt it was going to hurt when he removed himself once he was tired of her.

She offered no protest when he scooped her up in his arms. She snuggled against his chest and wrapped her arms around his neck as he carried her up the stairs. She briefly wondered why he didn't teleport them, but perhaps he enjoyed holding her as much as she enjoyed being held. Her room was still a disaster zone; the mattress had been tipped off the bed, and drawers and their contents were thrown around the room. He righted the rocking chair and placed it in the corner, gently setting her down in it. "Hold on a sec," he told her, then was a blur before her eyes as he set the room straight. In under a minute, the room was back as it should have been.

"Wow." She was impressed.

"Can't guarantee all your clothes are in the right places," he grinned, reaching for her, and plucking her out of the rocking chair and onto the bed in under a second.

Pinning both of her wrists above her head with

one hand, he lay along the length of her, careful not to crush her with his weight.

"You are the most beautiful woman," he whispered.

"Pfft," she scoffed, "I've seen who you hang out with Zak, and I'm no supermodel."

"No, you're not. You're real. You're beautiful on the inside and out. And. You. Taste. So. Damn. Sweet." He punctuated with kisses.

Opening her mouth to him, she raised one leg to run her foot along the back of his leg, drawing a groan from the back of his throat.

"I'll never hurt you." He spoke into her mouth, the words hot and arousing.

"Yes, you will. You may not mean to, but you will nevertheless."

"I'm not like you think I am. You think I fuck and leave, that I notch 'em up on my bedpost. Rumors of my prowess have been greatly exaggerated."

His words penetrated the lust-filled haze fogging her mind. How did he know she thought she was another notch on his bedpost? She tensed beneath him.

"You read my mind!" she accused, pulling at her wrists. He held firm, pulling back to put a little space between them but keeping her pinned beneath him on the bed.

"Couldn't help it. It came with your blood." He shrugged, not apologetic in the least.

"You bastard. That is just plain fucking rude. Get off me." She bucked and twisted, trying to dislodge him.

"Sweetheart, you moving like that is no incentive for me to get off you."

"Fuck you, asshole," she snarled, anger replacing the passion that had been thrumming through her veins only moments before. How dare he? How fucking dare he! Her private thoughts. Her dreams. Her secrets. *Fucking jerk.*

She struggled and twisted under him, growling, and cursing. He pressed more firmly against her, trapping her beneath him. Recalling every combat move she knew, she repeatedly attempted to turn the tables and gain the upper hand. Unfortunately, he knew every damn move and was prepared for every single one.

Eventually, she stopped struggling, begrudgingly accepting that it was useless. And she was utterly pissed about that too.

"I can't believe you did that to me."

"It wasn't intentional, although I won't lie, I

knew there was a chance I'd be able to read you when I drank your blood," he said softly as he brushed his lips over her forehead.

"The point is, I didn't want you to. My thoughts are mine. You had no right."

"I know." He gently kissed her forehead once more, "And I don't blame you. But we need to talk."

"You know what? We really don't."

He kissed his way down her neck and across her shoulder.

"You're being coerced by vampires, Georgia."

"Like I hadn't noticed."

"Vampires who want something that I have. You need to know I have no intentions of handing it over."

"I never expected that you would."

"Then how did you think this was going to end? That they'll just walk away and accept defeat? That's not how it's going to go down, Georgia. You and Skye will end up with your throats torn out."

He felt her flinch, and a heavy sigh escaped him.

"I'm not trying to scare you—I'm trying to drum it into that stubborn head of yours that you can't do this on your own. I've known something was up from the day I met you, and I've been waiting for you to open up and tell me, hoping against hope that you'd trust me enough to ask for help."

"What, you kissing other women, probably sleeping with them as well, is meant to get me to open up to you?"

"You're right. That looked bad. It's not like that, I swear. I've wanted you since the first moment I laid eyes on you."

"Yeah, right," she scoffed, turning her face away from him to hide the hurt in her eyes. "Veronica told me you fucked her that night. She went to great pains to make sure I knew that. Did she really lie?"

He lifted his head, frowning, "Yes, she lied about that night. I promise you I have not had sex with her. Recently." Georgia's body tensed beneath him again, and he felt her breath hitch in her chest. Damn it, he'd never thought one lapse in judgment would have such far-reaching consequences. It had been hundreds of years since he'd been in an actual relationship with a woman. Louise. He'd loved her, she'd loved him, only she'd grown old and died. It had taken his heart a long time to heal from the loss. He'd begged her to let him turn her so they could spend eternity together, but she'd always denied him. She hadn't wanted to be a vampire. What he hadn't known then was that it wasn't necessary. All she'd needed to do was take a little of his blood regularly, and her lifespan would have been extended, with no need to turn her.

The feelings he was starting to develop for Georgia were achingly familiar, and he craved them. Craved to feel love and be loved in return. The day he'd first met Georgia, the sight of her, the scent of her, had overwhelmed him. She was...luscious. He craved the taste of her; he craved to touch her, to have her as his own.

"I know this is all weird to you, but I don't feel for Veronica that way. It was a mistake, kissing her, one I should have known better. I allowed my judgment to become clouded. It will never happen again."

Although her instincts told her he was being truthful, Georgia couldn't quite believe him.

"But you have slept with her. You two have a history."

He winced, "I've been her sire for nearly 200 years. When I first turned her in the early days, she was filled with lust—both sexual and for blood. It is interchangeable with vampires, and until they learn to control it, let's just say a lot of new vampires don't survive. She fed and slept with only me for the first six months of her vampiric life. I was the only one strong enough to stop her from accidentally killing who she fed on. As she learned more control, she took other donors and slept with others. Our physical relationship became less and less frequent. This did not bother me; I'm not in love with her. We used each other for sex and blood. I haven't touched her in over ten years."

"If it was just sex and blood, then why did she feel the need to throw that in my face?" She desperately wanted to believe him, she really did, but what's to say he felt the urge again, and she wasn't around. It sounded like Veronica was the 'go-to' girl.

"I don't know how it happened or how it got by without me noticing it, but it wasn't the same for Veronica. She developed true feelings for me. I had no idea. She hid it. Even though I could read her mind, she's learned to put up walls. That's what the kiss was about. I knew she was hiding something but couldn't get past the wall I found. Kissing her, the intimate contact, allowed me to breach at least one of her defenses. She had another, stronger wall that I couldn't get around, but what I did find alerted me to the fact that she'd been spiteful to you, that she wanted me for herself. She'd picked up on my interest in you, an interest that I'd never had for any other woman since I'd turned her, and she felt threatened."

"Do you think she's behind the shop fire and my house getting trashed?"

"No. I'm sorry I wasn't around earlier when that happened—I had business to attend to in Elen Hills. With Veronica. She'll stay there indefinitely. I saw things in her mind that didn't add up; I need to do some investigating, plus I don't want her around you, poisoning you against me. You're not a one-night stand to me, Georgia. You're so much more."

As he stared down at her with a hint of desperation in his eyes, he seemed so lost. He looked at her as if she was his lifeline, as if he really did need her. She felt some of her anger fizzle away.

He dropped his forehead to hers. "I know this vampire shit is fucked up, that it's a lot for you to take in, that you're under considerable stress, but I would never hurt you. Not intentionally, not ever. You're mine. And I protect what is mine."

Why did he have to say stuff like that and wear that vulnerable expression when she was trying to stay mad at him? But hearing him say these things, vowing not to hurt her, claiming her as his...it was hard to hold out against. Adding to that, he was now licking her neck with sensuous strokes of his tongue, making her melt beneath him.

"That sounds so sexist."

He chuckled, "Maybe so, but it's the truth, and I know you secretly like it. You started melting before I started doing this." His mouth moved against her neck again. He released her wrists, and she immediately combed her fingers through his hair.

"You are so good with that mouth."

Zak fused his lips with hers, taking her taste inside him, pouring his need for her into her mouth. She arched beneath him, wrapping her legs around his waist, so he was cradled intimately against the very core of her. It blew his mind.

"You are fucking unbelievable," he muttered into her mouth, rocking his hips against her, so his erection rubbed against her most sensitive spot.

"Ditto," she gulped. His hands went to her jeans, but she quickly stopped him. He raised his head, frowning. "Please don't ruin all my clothes! There's no need to tear them off me every single time, is there?" she pleaded teasingly. He relaxed, moving his weight off her to shed their clothes the more traditional way.

Finally naked, he pinned her to the bed once more, hands seemingly everywhere at once, brushing over her skin and heating her blood with every caress. He breathed hot words into her ear, telling her exactly what he was going to do to her, how he'd fuck her until she screamed. His mouth moved to her breasts, pulling her pert nipples into his mouth and laving them with his tongue while his hand ventured lower, not teasing this time but going straight to the heart of her.

She was so wet for him, so hot and tight. He pushed a finger inside her, and she groaned. Slowly he moved that finger in and out, matching the rhythm with his tongue on her nipple; she moaned and squirmed, pushing herself against his hand for more. He obliged, pushing another finger inside and twirling before pulling out to lightly brush against her clit. Her body jerked with the contact but chased his hand when he moved away. He chuckled, moving his mouth back up to hers and plundering her mouth as he pushed his fingers back inside her, feeling the tension build and climb within her, but not allowing her release, not yet.

She pulled her mouth away in frustration and panted, her body taut with need and the release that he could give her.

"Please," she begged, not too proud to beg for

the pleasure he could give her that was tantalizingly out of reach.

Zak removed his fingers and slowly and deliberately pushed his cock inside her, wanting her to feel every inch of him sink deeper and deeper. She felt amazing, so hot, wet, and tight around him; he'd never felt anything like it. "Mine. You're mine," he said against her lips. He withdrew very slowly, and then he slammed into her. He'd planned to go slow, but need blinded him, and he was pounding into her with deep thrusts. He abruptly pinched one nipple, pulling a gasp of pleasure mixed with pain from her. He cupped her breast with his hand and lowered his mouth to her nipple, sucking it hard and scraping the sensitive flesh with his teeth. Her muscles contracted around him, squeezing and milking his cock, and he knew he wasn't going to last much longer. God, how this woman brought him to his knees.

His mouth moved back up to her neck, his fangs sinking into her sweet soft flesh, and she constricted around him as she came, gasping and shuddering. With an answering groan, he exploded within her, ramming into her with rough thrusts, filling her with everything he had.

Georgia threw her head back and cried out, her

body bucking against his as her mind opened to him, and he felt his own pleasure echoed back at him. She held on tight, her arms and legs wrapped around him as they rode the pleasure together.

They sagged against each other, breathing heavily, when Zak whispered, "I've never felt as close to anyone as I did just now, with you."

She shuddered beneath him, eyes drifting open and blinking at him. "I think I felt you," she whispered, "your mind," she clarified when she felt his cock twitch inside her.

"You read my mind?"

"No. I couldn't see what you were thinking. But I felt you. I felt your emotions, I guess. I dunno. It was kinda weird. I think I felt your pleasure. And mine?" Zak cut off her words with a hot kiss, holding her tightly against him in wonder. They'd merged! His mind had never merged with another's in five hundred years of existence. He was elated—she truly was his; this stubborn, determined, sexy as hell woman was his. He wanted to shout it from the rooftops.

"We've merged," he whispered against her lips, dropping feather-light kisses across her face in total awe and wonder.

"We've what?"

"Merged. Our minds reached out and connected —tell me, was that the most mind-blowing orgasm you've ever had?"

She blushed, giving him his answer.

"You're mine," he claimed again, "this proves it. For you to connect with me like that? It's never happened before, Georgia. Ever. With anyone."

"Really?" she cocked an eyebrow, shocked and kinda thrilled that maybe she had that little bit of something extra his other women didn't. So what if she didn't have supermodel looks and a killer body; she could tap this guy's mind like he was tapping her ass! Cool.

"Oh yeah." He grinned, knowing what she was thinking without having to read her. She smiled back at him, caressing his face with her fingers before running them up into his hair to tug his mouth back to hers.

FOURTEEN

"Come on! You have to give me some details," Skye whined, glaring at her sister across the burnt-out ruin of their shop. The stench of smoke was overpowering, and they'd propped the front doors open to try and clear the air. The floor squelched underfoot, a combination of water and ashes—what an unholy mess.

"Let me just say, the guy has mooooooves." Georgia grinned, remembering how many times Zak had made love with her last night, orgasm after mind-blowing orgasm. She'd never experienced anything like it in her life; the man was insatiable. But since their merging, she'd had to admit to herself, no matter how reluctantly, that it was more than sex. They hadn't spent the night fucking. They'd spent the night making love, and that was the rub. She really did have feelings for him, could feel his feelings for her bouncing back at her, and while it was exhilarating and surreal, it was also slightly terrifying.

She didn't know why their minds had merged; perhaps it was her psychic abilities, mixed with his mind-reading abilities, that meant they'd recognized something of themselves in each other. It was also frustrating that he could genuinely read her mind in that state, yet she couldn't read his. But she did know he was telling her the truth about Veronica; of that, she had no doubt.

"I figured that from all the squeals and groans coming from your room last night!" Skye sulked.

"Yeah. Sorry 'bout that." Georgia shrugged, unrepentant. With a sigh, she surveyed her surroundings. "You know, I don't think anything is salvageable, Skye," she admitted. Skye also looked around; not a single piece was left, just scorched chunks of wood with a hinge or door handle remaining. The ceiling was black, but thankfully, they had a high ceiling that hadn't burnt. The walls would need some minor repairs, and of course, everything needed a good scrub and fresh coat of paint.

"Agreed." The insurance assessor had been through that morning and given them the go-ahead to start cleaning. Georgia was extremely grateful that Skye had the business savvy to get them an excellent insurance policy—the insurance was going to cover the repairs and refurbishment and the cleaning. And not just the shop but Skye's apartment too.

Skye pulled out her mobile and began making calls, arranging for a clean-up crew, and lining up quotes for painting and refitting. While they waited for the cleaning crew to arrive, they climbed the outside staircase at the back of the building to Skye's apartment to grab some clothes. Everything in the apartment reeked of smoke as well. The carpets and curtains would need to be cleaned, and the walls scrubbed if not repainted. They carted armfuls of clothes back down the stairs and dumped them in Georgia's truck—they all needed to be washed, so they might as well take them back to the farm.

By the time they'd dealt with the cleaning crew, who'd initially sent two people until they'd seen the scope of the job and had then quickly called in another three, it was getting late. They agreed they'd focus on getting the shop cleaned first so that repairs could begin, then the cleaners could move on to the apartment, therefore not holding up progress on the shop. Still, it was going to take a fair amount of time before they'd be open for business again. Not only did they have the refurbishment, but they were also out of stock. Skye would start scouring auctions and garage sales to find some pieces, and Georgia would be kept busy getting them ready for sale.

"We need to talk."

Georgia was in the kitchen making coffee when Zak spoke from behind her, making her jump. Cursing, she glared at him over her shoulder.

"Geez, Zak. Don't friggin' do that. I nearly had a heart attack," she complained, turning back to the coffee, annoyed.

"We still need to talk." He stepped forward and placed a quick kiss on the nape of her neck before coming to lean against the counter next to her.

"About?"

"Erik. Your deadline. Your possible betrayal of me."

"What?" she spun, staring at him in surprise, "I'm not going to betray you, Zak," she assured him, frowning that he would believe that of her.

"You wouldn't be the first." He looked bored, which confused her. Where was this coming from?

"Don't give me that shit," she growled, "You've read my mind. You know I wasn't going to steal your precious ring. Okay, I admit I did give it some thought at the start, but honestly, it's not like you wouldn't notice a ring suddenly disappearing from your finger."

"You still think you can handle this on your own? You still think you can take on Erik and his vamps and live to walk away?"

"Actually, no, I don't," Georgia conceded, stalking away from him, careful not to spill her coffee but giving him her stiff back at the same time.

Her admission seemed to have taken the wind out of his sails because he looked at her with his mouth open for a moment. Good, she thought smugly, sneaking a glance over her shoulder.

"You're annoyed that I didn't confide in you. That you found out by reading my mind."

"We have a connection, Georgia! You should have told me yourself. I'm not a monster. I would have understood."

"Yeah, but I didn't know that!" She dismissed him with a wave of her hand. "I hardly knew you. For all I knew, the easiest solution—for you—would have been to kill me." He went to argue with her, but she held her hand up to stop him. "No." Irritation bristled over her skin, followed by frustration and lust. God, he was so infuriating. And hot. And confusing.

Silence followed. Georgia refused to look at him, keeping her eyes on the cup of coffee cradled in her hands. He sat next to her and pried a hand away from the cup, holding it in his and gently stroking her palm.

"You're right," he admitted, "I'm pissed you didn't come to me of your own free will."

"But now you know. Can we move on?"

He nodded, releasing her hand.

"So Frank has been doing some intel on your friend Erik."

"He's not my friend."

"And it looks like he and his little band of merry followers have traced me here from Elen Hills, with the sole intention of getting their hands on the ring. Their first attempt in Elen Hills failed."

"First attempt?"

"You know my home was destroyed in Elen Hills, yes?" At her nod, he continued, "It was a demon attack. A very coordinated demon attack, which in itself is unusual 'cos they're not the organized type.

It looks like the demons teamed up with vampires, which again is unusual because they're sworn enemies."

"All because of this ring." She pointed to the ring in question. Zak spun it on his finger as they both looked at it.

"Demons believe the ring has the power to destroy all vampires. Then they'd have free reign at controlling the Earth."

"And would it? Would the ring really do that?"

"Possibly. There would have to be more to it; the ring on its own is of no use to anyone but with the right magic or spell, then yes, it has the power."

"And the vampires want it to wipe out the demons?" Georgia guessed, surprised when Zak shook his head.

"No. We think the vampires want the ring to awaken a Master Vampire who's been asleep for millennia. They believe he is the original vampire, a god. We still don't know how either side even heard of the ring; all we know is both sides want it. Although, the demons have backed off after the massacre in Elen Hills."

"Massacre?"

"We killed over 100 of them. That's a lot of demons to have in one area—they usually only travel and work together in groups of two or three. So to get a hundred of them to cooperate with each other? Interesting, to say the least. This is why we believe the vampires were working with them to build a demon army. Only we destroyed it."

"Oh. Right. So when you say 'we,' you were involved too? You were fighting, killing?"

"Yes. I'm no saint, Georgia. I may be half angel, but that doesn't necessarily make me some sort of golden angel that does no wrong. I fight, I kill, and I enjoy the battle. I'm five hundred years old—I've seen many battles throughout my time. I've taken lives and enjoyed the thrill of the fight."

"Why are you telling me this?" she whispered.

"Because this is boiling down into a fight—and you need to know it will probably get violent and bloody. You need to know I'm a warrior, and I will fight to protect what is mine...including you. I will not see you harmed in this, and I will not show mercy to my enemies."

"If this is all so monumental, why on earth did Erik pick me to get the ring? I'm weak in comparison to vampires and demons."

"Because you activated the ring when you found the first blade."

"First blade?"

"The knife. The dagger. The one you have so sneakily hidden in your workshop." He winked at her.

"I don't get why we're talking about all this if you already know!" she sulked.

"Because you need to know as well, and I want no more secrets between us. I saw how you found the blade, that your blood activated it. The connection between the blade and the ring was activated, which is how I found you. And they simply followed me."

Zak looked at her, "The ring cannot be forcibly removed from my finger. I either have to remove it willingly, or it can be removed if I'm dead." She didn't understand the look he was giving her.

"They know you're psychic, and there would be a chance I wouldn't be able to read you. Once they knew for sure, you were approached. I think they were hoping you'd be able to seduce the ring from me."

"Oh, that never occurred to me. I vaguely thought I'd try to steal it," she confessed. "You know, on the assumption, you took it off while showering or sleeping or something."

"I know."

"But..." she frowned, "how did they know you

couldn't read me? I mean, how did they know for sure? How was it confirmed?"

"Someone has to be on the inside. Someone from within has betrayed me...I think Veronica may be involved somehow. Since I can't read all of her mind anymore, I know she's putting a lot of effort into hiding something vital—something big."

"Fuck." Georgia murmured. "But then, why try and scare me away from you? Surely they wanted me to get closer?"

"I'm sure that was the plan, but they hadn't counted on Veronica's jealousy."

"Right." Georgia nodded absently while taking a sip of her coffee before her senses suddenly went haywire. Shoving her chair back, she quickly rose to her feet, alarmed.

"Vampires!" she hissed, sensing the breach around her house.

Zak disappeared outside and returned seconds later.

"It's Frank and the boys. They're doing a security check, and Cole and Kyan will be staying to keep an eye on the place."

"Guarding me?"

"Helping to protect you. And Skye," he added when he saw her start to rile up at the thought of someone constantly watching her every move. "They were keeping an eye on things before, but we needed them when we briefly returned to Elen Hills. That's when Erik saw his opportunity to trash this place—otherwise, he wouldn't have gotten near it."

The constant buzz of vampires so close was starting to give Georgia a headache. Still, she knew she'd rather have them around than not—even though their presence messed up her sensory field, so she wouldn't know if Erik arrived, she'd much rather have the vamps outside head him off before he could get to her. Or Skye.

Rubbing her temples, she breathed through the heavy tension in her mind—she'd eventually adjusted to being in a houseful of vampires at Zak's house; she could manage it here as well.

"Okay?" Zak watched her with concern; she'd lost color, and he didn't like it.

She nodded, "Headache." He replaced the fingers at her temples with his own, sending soothing tingles through her skin where he healed her pain.

"It is so amazing you can do that," she murmured in relief.

Frank knocked at the door, and Zak rose to let him in.

"Georgia," he nodded in greeting, and she nodded in return.

"Cole and Kyan are taking the night shift. Dainton and Heath will take the day—although they'll need to come inside if that's alright with you?" Frank looked at her. While vampires could get around during daylight hours, they couldn't withstand the sun for long.

"That's fine."

The two men continued to speak in hushed tones that she couldn't hear. They finished up, Frank leaving and Zak returning to sit beside her.

"I need to go and take care of a couple of things," he told her, stroking his thumb across the back of her hand.

"Ok."

"I need you to stay here. Inside." He saw her start to stiffen, "Please, Georgia, stay put." Seeing his frustration, she nodded her head. She could use an early night anyway, and she was sure she'd sleep better knowing Kyan and Cole were keeping Erik and his cronies away.

H eath, Aston, and Dainton were in the conference room waiting for him. Zak teleported with Frank directly into the room, knowing that's where the team would be.

Aston was tapping at his laptop, pulling up a map.

"And we are live!" he grinned. Zak moved behind him to see the screen. Two red dots were blinking on the map. They'd put GPS trackers in Georgia and Skye's mobile phones.

"Good work," Zak patted his shoulder, "just do not tell the ladies we are tracking them. I could do without the grief."

Aston typed a few commands, and another map

appeared on the screen with a single red blinking dot.

"And here we have the lovely Veronica." He indicated the screen with his hand. Dainton and Heath crowded around to see the screen as well.

"Where is she?" Dainton queried. Anton zoomed the map in closer. Veronica was not at the safe house where they'd left her. She was two hundred miles to the west. Zak frowned. She hadn't been in contact with him to tell him of her movements, and while he hadn't forbidden her from leaving the safe house, it wasn't the norm for one of his own not to keep him abreast of their movements.

"Do we have any more intel on her?" he asked Frank. It bothered him that he had to ask them to investigate one of their own; it hurt, even more, to think that she had, or was intending, to betray them all.

"We don't have anything to connect her directly to Erik. Yet. She's damn good at hiding whatever it is she's up to. And for her to be able to hide it so effectively from you? Someone has to have taught her that trick."

"Her blocking technique is very effective," Zak agreed. Although he'd tried several times to read Veronica's secrets, she'd still maintained that wall that he just hadn't been able to breach. What saddened him the most was that she'd felt the need to learn how to block him. He respected his people's privacy and didn't intrude on their minds.

He knew Veronica's behavior hurt the warriors as well. She was their sister. If she was in trouble, she could have turned to any one of them for help.

Zak took a seat at the conference table and listened as Frank updated them all on what they'd found on Veronica and Erik, which hadn't amounted to much. Lots of rumors, but nothing concrete. Aston turned on the television screen on the wall at the end of the table and hooked up his laptop. The screen flickered for a moment, and then they all saw a replication of Aston's laptop monitor. The picture on the screen was of Georgia's dagger.

"We do have news of the first blade, though," Aston told them. "Dainton, care to share what you found out?"

Dainton leaned forward in his chair, resting his elbows on the table.

"It's as we suspected. The blade has more of a role to play than simply awakening the ring."

Zak glanced down at the ring with its thin red line weaving around his finger.

"While the ring has the power to awaken the

original, the dagger has the power to end his life permanently. The legends tell us he cannot be killed, and this is backed up by many trying but none succeeding. Until the spell that was cast on him, that took him to eternal slumber. Still, slumber is not death. The witch that cast the spell was mighty, but as we know, when dealing with magic, you have to have balance. A loophole, if you will. So while her spell allows him to sleep, there is a loophole to awaken him and a loophole to kill him."

"Can anyone use the blade?" Heath asked.

"Anyone can 'use' it," Dainton nodded, "but whoever activated it, and therefore the ring, is the one who would have to wield the death blow for it to work."

"So if I were to stab the original one in the heart with the blade, he would not die? It would have to be Georgia?" Aston queried.

"Correct. The dagger can be used in battle without any special powers, but when it comes to killing the original? It was Georgia's blood that awakened it, and only she can wield it to kill him."

"How did it come to be here?" Zak asked.

"Legend has it that after the spell was cast and the ring and dagger blessed, the dagger was taken by a young witch and hidden. On her deathbed, that witch disclosed the location with the instructions that it was to be handed to another and hidden again. The cycle was to repeat itself. The dagger has changed hands many times, so the hiding place kept changing, and the keeper of the dagger was soon lost track of. It soon became nothing more than folklore."

"What's the plan, Boss?"

"Protect the girls."

"I have an idea," Frank spoke up.

"Let's hear it."

"Train Georgia. Train her to be a warrior and to use the blade."

"No."

"You're leaving her vulnerable, Zak. That girl has moves; she'd be up for this. We've seen the various footage of her and the pub brawls over the years. She loves a good fight. Why not train her, and make her a better fighter?"

"Why not ask her what she wants?" Anton spoke up.

"Yeah," they all conspired against him. *Damn it.*

Georgia jumped at the opportunity.

"Fight like a warrior? Shit yeah!" she practically bounced in front of him.

"We'll teach you to fight, but only so you can protect yourself; you're not joining the Warriors. There's a difference," Zak growled at her, still not happy with the turn of events, even though he reluctantly admitted it made sense.

"You just don't want a girl on your team."

"I had a girl on my team. Didn't turn out so well."

"Oh yeah. *Her*." Georgia's lip curled in disgust. "Anyway, I don't want to be a warrior, but if you can help me kick Erik's ass, I'm all in."

"Training will be...brutal. There will be pain, lots of it."

"Will you quit trying to talk me out of it," she sighed, exasperated. "Let's do this already."

THEY CIRCLED EACH OTHER, knees bent. Georgia had watched the first couple of rounds Zak had demonstrated with Heath. Now it was her turn. No problem, she had this. She knew his tells, how he'd feint to the left and then suddenly swing his leg out, sweeping her feet out from under her. Or when it looked like he was going for a body punch and head-butted her instead. Oh yeah, she knew what to look for. He thought he was going to have her down to the ground and pinned in a matter of seconds, but Georgia had been a scrapper since she was a kid. He'd warned he wouldn't go easy on her, and she wanted that, didn't want any special treatment, just needed the training required to take down a vampire without getting herself killed.

He came at her, and she dodged, rolling to avoid the punch that should have connected with the side of her head. Missed! Surprise flashed through his eyes as he regained his balance and turned on her again. This time his left arm came toward her, aiming a fist at her stomach, but she was ready for him, grabbing his fist with both hands and using it as leverage to jump when his leg swept under her. His own momentum sent him staggering away from her.

"Minx," he growled, lips twitching. She danced away, light on her feet.

He came at her again, but she wasn't quite fast enough, his fist landing on her shoulder rather than jaw. She spun, her whole arm going numb. She wouldn't be surprised if her shoulder was dislocated. Zak stopped and straightened, frowning at her, opened his mouth to speak.

"Don't you dare fucking apologize!" she hissed, wiping sweat from her face. "Let's finish this!"

The guys cheered, watching from the sidelines as she danced and twirled, avoiding punches and kicks, landing a few of her own. Her shoulder wasn't dislocated, and the feeling had come back in a rush of the most extreme case of pins and needles she'd ever experienced.

She was tiring and drenched in sweat. She'd have been pissed if Zak had looked fresh as a daisy, but he was sporting a sheen of perspiration across his forehead. He hadn't landed her on her ass straight away, which filled her with pride, but she knew she wasn't going to be able to topple him. Not without fighting dirty. Just so happened 'fighting dirty' was her middle name.

She was panting, picking herself up from where she'd slid some ten feet away. Dusting herself off, she eyed him. He watched her, eyes glinting. He'd learned her tells as well, but she'd bet he hadn't seen this move before. Closing in on him, she grabbed the bottom edge of her shirt and lifted, catching her bra as she went; she flashed him, wiggling her breasts.

Crunch! Her fist connected with his nose. Whoomph. Another fist in the stomach as his hands had automatically flown to his face. Doubled over, she brought her elbow down on the back of his neck, dropping him to his knees with a groan. She raised her foot, resting her boot against his shoulder, and pushed, toppling him sideways.

A whoop went up around her. And she turned to face them, a grin on her face.

"You did it!" Cole cheered, high-fiving her.

"Not bad for a human chick," from Dainton. High praise indeed.

Zak rolled to his feet, nose already healed. He was grinning at her, pride in his eyes.

"Good job." Little words, but she soaked them in, delighted. Who knew being such a hell-raiser as a teenager would actually come in handy one day? As pleased as she was with her victory, the throbbing in her hand was making its presence felt.

"I think I broke something besides your nose." She held her hand up in front of her. Without hesitation, Zak covered her hand with his own. She hissed in a breath when the bones of three knuckles slipped back into place with an audible crack, but then the warm tingling started, erasing the pain and healing the bruised tissue.

The boys were amped up, so Zak tussled with them while Georgia took a break and got her breath back. Then it was on to training with knives. Zak had instructed Kyan to tutor her; he was the best among them for blades.

Because her dagger was made of silver and therefore deadly to vampires, Kyan gave her a substitute for practicing with its blade made of steel. He had her practice on a straw-filled hessian sack to get her used to handling the knife. Then it was throwing. Finally, what she'd been itching to try, live training.

She stood facing him now, breath rasping in and out of her lungs, skin sheened in sweat, but she would not back down. Crouched, knife held confidently in hand, she watched him. He was motionless before her, eerily so, but then she'd gotten used to that. It was a weird vampire thing. Her eyes scoured for his tell, a twitch or a blink that gave him away. There! That blink meant he was about to pounce. Just as he began to move, she cut him off, leaping out of the way and slicing with the blade simultaneously. The knife left a trail of red across his stomach, and he looked down in surprise. She'd nailed him. His eyes narrowed dangerously, and he mimicked her crouch. It was on like Donkey Kong. He pounced, she lunged, and the dance continued, movements fast and fluid until suddenly he was on top of her, and white-hot pain shot through her abdomen. Her hands clutched at her stomach, and she felt wet stickiness ooze through her fingers.

"Ah fuck," Kyan cursed, springing up from her. They both looked to where the knife was protruding from her stomach, the scent of her blood filling the air.

"Georgia!" Zak roared, materializing by her side.

"Not his fault," she breathed, knowing Zak was going to have Kyan's hide for this.

"No? I beg to differ." Anger radiated from him.

"Baby. Please," she sighed, pain coloring her words, "let's not fight about this. Can you help me? It really fucking hurts."

"Sorry, sweetheart. Brace yourself; it's going to hurt more before it feels better." He pulled the knife from her flesh with his jaw clenched, and she hissed, her body stiffening. His eyes met hers as he placed his hand over the wound, her blood warm against his palm. The sting was worse this time, and her eyes rolled back into her head; it felt like he'd let loose with a white-hot poker to her insides. She was dancing on the edge of darkness when the pain finally left, and the soothing tingle took its place.

Like the first time he'd healed her, once he was done, she felt like a wet noodle, totally drained.

"Why do I feel so weak?" she murmured as he swung her up into his arms.

"The worse the injury, the weaker you feel after the healing," he explained. He eyed Kyan. "We shall talk of this, warrior."

"I apologize, Sire." Kyan bowed his head, "Her injury was an accident. She'd bested me," he indicated the bloodstain across his own abdomen, "and I reacted instinctively."

"See?" Georgia piped up sleepily, "I bested him. 'Cos, I'm the bestest." Both warriors couldn't help but grin at the pride in her voice. Then she passed out. Shaking his head in resignation, Zak teleported her home, laying her gently on her bed to sleep it off.

CHAPTER
SEVENTEEN

Frank's phone buzzed. He glanced down at the text message.

"We've got trouble. Erik and his goons have turned up at Georgia's. Only he's been busy recruiting; he's got about twenty vamps with him."

"Shit!" Heath muttered, jumping to his feet, quickly followed by Aston and Dainton. They quickly armed themselves with knives and swords before taking formation, side by side, with one hand on the shoulder of the warrior beside them. Zak stood at the end. As soon as Frank's hand fell onto his shoulder, he teleported them all.

All hell had broken loose at Georgia's. Cole and Kyan had tried their best to keep the vamps from getting inside the house, but there were too many of them. Zak had teleported to her front garden, dropped the troops, and immediately teleported inside the house. It was the quickest way of finding her.

Georgia was fending off a vamp who had her pinned against the lounge room wall. Blood was running from a gash in her arm, but she was giving as good as she got with the vamp who was trying to rip her throat out. Zak pulled him off her and sent him flying across the room.

"You ok?" He quickly looked her up and down, searching for signs of a serious injury. Despite being battered and bruised, she appeared ok. Her quick nod assured him of this, and he turned his back on her to fight off the vamp who'd just picked himself up off the floor.

Within minutes Zak had torn his throat out. Another vamp was there to take his place, and the battle raged on. Zak kept half of his mind on Georgia, ensuring she was behind him, and no one reached her. Bodies continued to pile up until finally, the remaining vamps retreated.

"Well, ain't this a fuckin' mess," Georgia mumbled from behind him. He spun, hands reaching for her and pulling her into his embrace.

"You're not hurt?" He badly needed her

reassurance that she was alright. As he held her tightly, he heard the warriors securing prisoners and searching the grounds for survivors. Frank rushed in and murmured hurried words in Zak's ear.

He looked down at the woman in his arms.

"It's about Skye."

She froze. After a surprised silence, fear crossed her features.

"He took her?" she managed.

"Yeah."

The color drained from her face a moment before she panicked. She pushed at him, trying to get free.

"Easy," he said softly, holding her tighter. He pushed her back against the wall, using his body to still her movements. She was shaking against him. With a frustrated groan, she stopped fighting.

"Zak." Her voice cracked with emotion, and tears were in her eyes.

"Listen to me." He kept his voice calm and level, "First up, you are not running out of here on your own. We can get your sister back, and we're here to help you."

She listened, though fear and hysteria were in her gaze. He smoothed away the tears brimming from her eyes and kissed her.

Frank was barking orders behind him.

"Dainton and Heath, get rid of these bodies. Cole and Kyan, prisoners back to the homestead. Aston back to command central, check that GPS."

Activity burst around them at vampiric speed. Zak teleported Aston and Georgia back to the conference room, where Aston got to work immediately on tracking Skye. They were lucky; she had her phone with her. Georgia didn't bat an eyelid that they'd bugged their phones. The red dot that was Skye was moving across the map with astonishing speed.

"We have to get after her!" Georgia cried, pulling on Zak's arm.

"Sweetheart, calm," he soothed. "Erik won't kill her; he doesn't have what he wants yet," Zak explained. "They need the ring to awaken the original. I have the ring. Not you, nor Skye. He knows if he kills her, he has no chance of getting the ring from me. She is merely a bargaining chip."

"Then why take her, why not me?" she cried, frightened and frustrated and wanting badly to stamp her foot.

"I think it was a smash and grab attempt at either of you. He already knew you could defend yourself, and there was a slight chance you'd get yourself killed in the attempt to snatch you. Skye was the softer target. If he could have got you both, well, that would have been icing on the cake for him."

Georgia sank into a chair at the conference table, eyes bruised. Aston stiffened in his seat before raising his eyes to Zak.

"Boss, perhaps you could attend to her wounds," he indicated Georgia's bleeding arm with a nod of his head, "I'm getting a tad distracted over here," he grumbled, fangs sliding out.

"Apologies, my friend." Zak cursed himself for not healing her sooner. Not only must her arm be painful, but the scent of her blood was not a temptation he wanted to put in front of his warriors. Spinning her chair to face him, he laid a hand over her bleeding arm. The familiar sting of pain, followed by the soothing white glow, soon had her torn flesh knitted back together. Big strong hands gently cupped her face and healed away her bruises, his eyes intent as he scanned her body for any other pains.

"Thank you," she whispered.

Georgia closed her eyes and tried to reach out to her sister. Nothing. Still, an empty space where her sister's light should have been. Not death, but not life either. Georgia shuddered at the thought of what was about to befall her. This was all her fault. If she'd fessed up to Zak in the first place, all of this could have been avoided.

"Stop blaming yourself."

"You can't read my mind, remember?" she grumbled.

"I don't need to to know that you're beating yourself up over this. This is not your fault."

Georgia pushed up out of her chair and began pacing. Zak watched with hooded eyes.

"Looks like they've stopped," Aston broke the silence.

"Where?" Zak and Georgia spoke together.

"Crystal Lakes. It's an abandoned winery— should only take about an hour by car."

"Why not just teleport us there?" Georgia asked Zak.

"I can only teleport to places I have been. I need to picture my destination in my mind first, visualize where I want to be, for it to work."

It was midnight when they hit the road, piled into two SUVs. Zak had tried to talk Georgia into staying behind, staying safe, but she wouldn't have a bar of it. This mess was her fault, and she had to do what she could to fix it. She'd retrieved the dagger from its hiding place in her workshop and shoved it into her boot, and she wouldn't hesitate to use it; the lessons Kyan had been giving her had helped, and while she could still use some more practice on throwing and actually hitting her target, she'd picked up enough to improve her chances when it came to hand-to-hand combat.

The warriors discussed battle strategy while Georgia looked out the window at the dark night, her human eyes making out nothing of the landscape they passed. She noticed the small townships they drove through before nothing but black landscape again. The countryside surrounding Redmeadows was beautiful, full of small townships built to accommodate local wineries. Some of their wines were famous worldwide, which gave her a sense of pride.

She'd never heard of Crystal Lakes, but then Aston had said it was abandoned, so that was probably why.

The SUVs slowed in the middle of the black night, finding an almost hidden track off the main highway. Turning off their lights, they crept along. Georgia peered outside but couldn't make out much. After a couple of miles on the rough, overgrown track, shadows of buildings appeared. Still, Georgia could see that they were derelict, practically falling down as they got closer. No one had lived or worked in this vineyard for many years.

The SUVs pulled to a halt, and the warriors disembarked, disappearing into the night. Georgia slowly followed, Zak by her side.

"They're not here," she said sadly.

"They're not far. We didn't expect them to be at the winery itself, way too easy for them to be found or disturbed. The boys are searching; they'll pick up the trail."

True to his word Cole soon appeared in front of them.

"On foot from here. See those hills?" he turned and pointed. Georgia could see nothing but blackness, but Zak nodded. "They took her that way. Possibly a cave or some sort of underground facility. The signal dropped out." Georgia sucked in a breath. Cole put a reassuring hand on her shoulder, "Don't worry, we don't need the signal this close. We can track 'em ourselves."

They set off on foot, the vampires slowing their speed to accommodate her human pace. Georgia frowned as they walked between the old dead vines. While she tried to keep her footfalls quiet, she sounded like a herd of elephants compared to the vampires with her, who seemed to glide across the ground without a sound. Frank halted them.

"You need to stay here," he told her. "It's not safe for you to go any further."

"No way! I'm coming with you," she protested.

"Georgia, please," Zak grabbed her hand, "We need to focus on getting your sister out of there alive. You will slow us down and be a distraction we don't need. Wait here. Please."

Frustrated and annoyed, she sullenly nodded. Zak led her to a large tree and positioned her behind the trunk, deep in the shadows.

"Stay. Put." He growled.

She watched as they moved to what appeared to be a cave entrance in the side of the hill. Her eyes had adjusted to the darkness, and she could just make out their shapes before they disappeared into the gaping black pit. She waited all of two minutes before creeping across the ground as quietly as she could and following them into the black void.

Turns out what appeared to be a cave was, in fact, an old mine shaft, held up with massive timber beams. She shuddered to think how rotten they were and how imminent a cave-in was. The first few feet were total darkness, and she kept a hand against the wall as she shuffled along. The tunnel slowly curved, and beyond the curve, sporadic lanterns had been stretched along the tunnel, casting just enough light to see by.

The tunnels were cold and dry, the dirt beneath her feet kicking up dust and making her want to sneeze. She peered ahead, seeing no one. She strained her ears, but silence greeted her. She slowly made her way along, following the patches of light. Tunnels branched off from the main one she followed, but they remained in darkness. She figured she was heading in the right direction if she followed the light.

Finally, she was close enough to make out sounds, like a scuffling. She quickened her pace, reaching into her boot and pulling out the dagger, the weight a comforting presence in her hand.

She reached the end of the tunnel, which opened out into a large cavern. She could hear shouting, the yells echoing around her, and had been expecting to see the battle before her, yet the chamber was empty. With a frown, she crept through the entry and stepped sideways, keeping her back to the cold rock of the wall. She couldn't tell which way the sounds were coming from, but they were close. She couldn't see any other exits from the cavern, so she started shuffling around the exterior, hoping to come across some sort of hidden exit. They couldn't have disappeared, and the lights had only led in this direction. There was only one light in the cavern, in the center.

There! A small opening, rising to the level of her hip. She squatted down and peered in. Sure enough, light glowed through the small tunnel, and the noises were definitely coming from there. She'd have to crawl through; goodness knows how Zak and his warriors had fit!

On her hands and knees, she crawled her way through the opening of the short tunnel, which led to another cavern, not as big as the first, but this one was well lit, with several lamps strategically placed on the rock floor. She'd noticed from her protesting knees that the ground was no longer soft dirt but hard rock.

She crawled through and, staying low, plastered herself against the jutting rocks to the left of the entrance. No one had noticed her; they were all engaged in punching the snot out of each other. Blades flew, fists connected with flesh, blood, and grunts filled the air. She shivered, keeping her own dagger close to her chest.

Where was Skye? Between the bloody bodies, she spotted her across the cavern; Erik had her pinned against his chest with an arm around her throat, using her as a human shield against Zak. Zak was positively glowing with anger. The two vampires were at a standoff. If she could just distract Erik, that would allow Zak to lunge and hopefully get Skye out of his clutches uninjured.

It was pointless to create a distraction from so far away; one of the lesser vamps could quickly pick her off, and it would all have been for nothing. In the center of the cavern was a massive rock formation, about the size of a car. The top appeared flat but had a long rock formation along it. Perfect cover.

She waited for an opening and darted across the floor, keeping low. She pressed up against the rock, keeping her head down so she couldn't be seen. Vampires continued to fight around her, but no one had noticed her yet, which amazed her. She continued to shuffle along the rock, cursing the roughness as it scraped against her bare arms. She came around the end, positioned herself behind Erik. Closing her eyes, she centered herself, taking a couple of deep breaths before raising her arm and throwing the dagger. She watched, breath held, as the dagger flew through the air. A few more inches and it would be buried between Erik's shoulder blades. Then he moved! *What? No. No, no, no.* She watched in horror as the blade sailed past him. Into Zak.

In horror, she watched, the blade pushing through muscle and flesh until it came to a halt, hilt deep in the center of his chest.

She rushed forward, past Erik, her arms outstretched to Zak; his arms instinctively came up to grab hers, keeping them both balanced.

She raised her terrified eyes to his, and he looked at her in wonder, blood leaking from his wound to start trickling down his chest. *Oh my god, what had she done*? His face paled, and his hands slid from her arms to flop at his sides. His knees began to crumble, and his eyes rolled into the back of his head.

"ZAK!" she screamed, "No, no, no!"

"Well, well, well," Erik drawled from behind her, "I couldn't have planned it better myself."

"It was meant to be you!" Georgia yelled at him, struggling to turn her body that felt as if it was weighed down with wet concrete.

A loud thud indicated Zak had hit the floor. Georgia turned on Erik in a rage, intent on hurting him in any way she could, despite having no weapon aside from her anger and grief, grief that hadn't fully materialized since her brain couldn't fathom what had just happened. She launched at him, and he simply laughed, a solid punch to the side of her head sending her flying. She hit the ground hard, her cheekbone slamming into the rock with a loud crack. Her vision blurred as she blinked her eyes, trying to get her bearings, but the room was spinning, and her head hurt.

She closed her eyes for a minute. When she opened them again, she could focus on Zak, laying only a few feet away, eyes open and unseeing, staring up into nothing, her dagger protruding from his chest. A chest that was no longer breathing. Exactly as he'd appeared in her vision.

She groaned, the pain from her head injury nothing compared to the pain tearing her heart in two. *She'd killed him.*

The sounds of battle dimmed around her, and she realized the fighting had moved down the small tunnel and into the larger cavern. Only Erik, Skye, and Georgia remained. And Zak's body.

Georgia tried to pull herself up, but the pain in her head was debilitating. The cavern spun around her, and she gave up, laying her face against the rough cold ground again, ignoring the burning and throbbing in her cheek.

She watched through blurry eyes as Erik spun

Skye to face him. He spoke to her, his voice low so Georgia couldn't make out the words. Skye stopped struggling and looked into Erik's hypnotic gaze. With a nod, she stepped away from him, moving across the cavern to kneel at Zak's side.

"Skye," Georgia groaned, "don't do this. Fight him. Please..."

Skye's eyes were blank, not indicating she'd even heard her sister speak. She lifted Zak's lifeless hand and slid the ring from his finger. Tears stung Georgia's eyes. No movement from Zak, not so much as a twitch. He'd gone. Left her. And she was the one who'd sent him on his way. Oh god. Her tears pooled on the floor beneath her, and she struggled to catch her breath. The pain in her chest burned, her heart hurting with each beat.

Skye stood, the ring resting in the palm of her hand. She offered it to Erik.

"Well done, my dear. Now come and stand here." He indicated a spot next to the stone slab in the cavern's center.

Erik placed the ring on the crumbled pile of rocks on the slab, then began a chant in words Georgia couldn't understand. He took Skye's wrist in his hand and brought it to his mouth, fangs gleaming. He tore her wrist open, blood dripping from his fangs as he held her dripping hand over the pile of crumbled rocks.

Georgia stirred. Her sister wasn't in pain. Whatever trance Erik had her in had spared her that, but by the way the blood was pulsing from her torn wrist, he'd severed an artery. She was going to bleed out in minutes. Georgia couldn't lose them both. Struggling to her knees, the room swaying and dipping around her in dizzying circles, she crawled the few feet to Zak's body. Distracted, she gently touched his cheek.

"I love you," she whispered, a tear landing on his cheek, then trickling down his face as if it was he who was crying. Tearing her eyes from him, she wrapped her shaking fingers around the dagger and pulled it free from his chest with a slurping noise. Nausea rolled in her stomach.

Erik was still chanting, but he'd moved behind Skye to support her sagging body; the blood that had been pulsing from her wrist was slowing to a trickle.

Georgia struggled to her feet, stumbling forward and catching herself on the rock slab to keep her balance. The dagger slipped from her grasp and clanged to the floor, but she didn't notice. The pile of rubble on the slab had moved. Changed shape.

What she had thought was a pile of rock...was slowly transforming into the form of a man. Her foggy brain tried to make sense of what she was seeing. Skye's blood was dripping into the man's mouth. His body had changed from rock into a kind of mummified state. The skin looked dry and brittle, but she could see clearly defined limbs and torso. She could make out shadowed eye sockets, a nose, and hollowed-out cheekbones as his face started to take shape. On his chest sat Zak's ring.

Erik stopped chanting and threw Skye's body to the ground behind him, blood still trickling slowly from the wound in her wrist. Georgia didn't know how long her sister had or if she could even save her.

"You can't," Erik told her, meeting her eyes before looking back down at the Master Vampire who was awakening before him.

Dazed, Georgia watched too, her world dipping and swaying, unable to make sense of what was before her. The vampire on the stone slab moved, his limbs twitching as blood began circulating through his system once more. Then in a rush of movement, he was up, his skeletal hands gripping Georgia by the shoulders and dragging her to him. His mouth had taken shape, four-inch fangs protruding from dry, cracked lips. Then his fangs sank into her neck, and she screamed, the pain horrifying as his fangs pierced her flesh. He guzzled at her neck, pulling in great gulps of her blood, and she knew she was about to die here. At least she'd get to be with Zak and Skye again, she thought as her eyes fluttered closed and the darkness took her.

Rhys frowned at the recorded message telling him the cell phone he'd called was either switched off or out of service. Shoving his mobile back into his pocket, he surveyed the front of the burnt-out store, his sensitive nose picking up the faint scent of a vampire over the heavy stench of smoke and wet ash. First the fire, now he couldn't get a hold of either of the Pearce sisters. His gut told him something was going on. Something bad.

Stepping into the store, he watched the clean-up crew for a moment before drawing another deep breath. He couldn't be one hundred percent certain, but he didn't think the vampires had been in the shop. Just outside. Although, any traces of them could have been covered by the fire itself. Striding across the floor, he made his way to the back entrance and up the stairs to Skye's apartment. That, too, had suffered smoke damage, but thankfully he couldn't detect any vampires inside.

It was just after ten. He'd been expecting either Skye or Georgia, possibly both, to be here. It was strange that they weren't. He knew how much the shop meant to them, how devastated they'd been when it had been torched. And it had been arson; of that, there was no doubt. It was out of character for both girls not to be here, supervising the clean-up and making plans to get the place up and running again. And giving him grief about finding the bastard who'd done this.

A shiver crept up his spine. If anything happened to those girls... he didn't want to think about it. More to reassure himself than due to any sense of them really being in danger, he returned to his patrol cruiser and headed out to Georgia's farmhouse. He smiled to himself—Georgia would give him a serve for worrying about them like a mother hen. She'd lecture him that she was big enough and ugly enough to take care of herself, thank you very much. Even though it was him, she'd call when she inevitably found herself in trouble or drunk and needed a ride home.

He thought back over the last few weeks and just how often she'd roused him from a deep sleep to drive her drunken ass home. A little too often for comfort, he acknowledged. Something had been going on with her lately, even before she'd gotten involved with Zak Goodwin, and just the thought of the vampire had Rhys's hackles rising. He told himself it was just his protective streak that his role of protector to the two girls was kicking in. Still, he'd spent some time reflecting in the bottom of a beer bottle himself and admitted there was a twinge of jealousy there too.

Pulling to a halt in Georgia's driveway, he climbed out, almost staggering at the scent that greeted him. Vampires. Lots of them. He approached the house, hurrying, when he noticed the front door standing open.

"Georgia? Skye?" he called out, hand resting on his gun as he approached. Silence greeted him. Something was definitely wrong. Moving with stealth, he climbed the stairs and pressed his back to the wall by the door. Freeing his gun, he raised it to his chest.

"Police!" he shouted. "Nobody move!" He swung

into the doorway and froze, gun aimed, scanning the room. Stepping inside, he noted the broken furniture, blood, but no bodies. Quickly he worked his way through the house.

"Police! Call out!" he kept repeating, praying that Georgia and Skye had found a safe place to hide and weren't game to come out.

Upstairs he checked the bedrooms, frowning when he saw the broken window and torn fly screen in the spare room where Skye would have been staying. He looked down through the window. Had she been taken? Why would vampires kidnap a human? Why not kill her here? Drain her and leave? Because that wasn't what they wanted her for, he surmised. She was needed. For what?

Frustrated, he hurried back down the stairs to the living room, crouching and examining the floor. He could scent Georgia here. She'd been injured, had bled. But of all the blood pooled on the floor, only a drop or two were human. Had she been taken too? Why? Why would vampires take two human girls by force? He knew they could glamor humans into doing whatever they wanted, so why do it this way? Was it Georgia's psychic ability that made her a target? He knew she couldn't read vampires—they were already dead after all, but maybe 'they' didn't know that?

Reaching for his radio, he called it in. Either way, two human women were missing. He knew when they dusted for prints, they'd never find a match, just like the blood specimens would come back as being contaminated or some such thing, explaining away what the human police officers couldn't fathom. That vampires, shifters, and werewolves did exist.

He went back outside and leaned against his cruiser to wait. Pulling out his cell phone, he dialed his alpha, Hayden Donovan.

"Rhys. What's up?"

"We've got trouble, Hayden. Vampire trouble."

"What's happened?"

"I'm not one hundred percent sure yet, but it looks like Georgia and Skye have been taken. Forcefully. Their shop was firebombed the other night. Now their house is trashed. Vamp blood everywhere."

"Vamp blood? Fighting amongst themselves?"

"Georgia's been seeing Zak Goodwin. I'd say he and his crew were here to help the girls. It's my best guess. I'm going to explore that angle, go and talk to him, see if I can find out what happened, but I need to keep that side of it off the record."

"I don't like you getting involved in vampire business, Rhys."

"I can't *not* do anything. It's Georgia and Skye we're talking about."

Hayden sighed. "Fine. I know you're close to the girls. But don't bring this fight to our doorstep Rhys —we don't want a war between the vampires and wolves. Especially over humans."

"Noted."

CHAPTER

NINETEEN

The pain was everything. Every breath hurt, every limb hurt, her internal organs hurt. With a groan, she cracked open her eyes, only to be met with darkness. Was she still in the cave? She flexed her fingers, feeling the floor beneath her. Yes, it was a floor. Cold and hard but definitely the floor of a building, not rock and dirt.

She struggled to sit up, her head pounding. Nausea rolled, and she stilled, not sure if she was about to hurl. Eventually, her stomach settled, and she managed to sit up and prop her back against the wall behind her. Not only was her head throbbing, so was her neck. Probing her neck with her fingers, she discovered Erik had literally torn a chunk out of her. No neat fang holes for her! He hadn't drained her, and she wasn't sure if she should be grateful or not. A wave of dizziness washed over her, and she pulled up her knees, resting her forehead against them.

"I know you're awake in there," Erik's voice taunted. She spun her head around, wincing as the movement broke open the raw wound on her neck. A door opened, and a pool of light flooded the room. She could see now she was in some sort of cell. The walls were brick with no windows; the floor was concrete, and the cell was completely empty except for Georgia.

"I'd not intended for you to live this long, my sweet Georgia." Erik sauntered into the room, pulling on a cord from the ceiling. The light stung her eyes from the naked light bulb dangling from the ceiling.

"But the Master enjoyed your blood so much, he insisted we bring you along and at least try and keep you alive. For a little while, at least. He has been in slumber for too long. Who am I to deny him the ambrosia of your blood?"

"What?" Georgia rasped, her throat dry, her brain foggy.

"Don't you remember, sweet child? You kindly dispatched that damn angel vampire abomination, and your sister gave the master the lifeblood he needed to awaken."

Georgia tried to lunge at him, but she was weak, and the effort to move hurt more than it should have. She knelt in a puddle at his feet.

"Oh, I do love your spirit. I will love it, even more, when I break it!"

"Asshole," Georgia muttered.

"Enough, I grow tired of this. Master wants to see you." Grabbing her arm, he dragged her to her feet, holding her upright when her knees sagged beneath her.

He dragged her along a dark corridor before pushing her up a flight of stairs. They emerged into a kitchen, the windows above the sink reflecting nothing but the night sky outside.

Erik kept a painful grip on her arm as he led her through what appeared to be a vast and very expensively decorated house. He came to a halt before a set of arched doors with beautiful carvings depicting a garden scene. He raised his free hand and knocked.

"Enter."

The door swung open seemingly by itself. A large hand placed between her shoulder blades pushed her into the room. Georgia didn't know what she had been expecting, but it wasn't this. The room was gorgeous. Bookcases lined one wall, stretching all the way to the cathedral ceiling. Sofas and reading nooks with antique armchairs called forth a cozy and relaxing place to read. A massive fireplace dominated the end of the room, so large she bet she could stand up in it, and off to one side stood a magnificent mahogany desk, complete with an antique lamp. Behind that desk sat a man Georgia hadn't seen before. But she felt him; his vampiric power positively sizzled her nerve endings.

Erik released her, and she stood, trembling as the vampire rose from his seat and approached her. He was an inch or two taller than her, his skin so pale it was white, his eyes glowing red and his hair as black as midnight. She couldn't really tell, but she thought it was pulled back into a ponytail. He wore a crisp suit and was stunningly handsome.

"Please," he grabbed her hand and pressed his lips to the back of it, "allow me to introduce myself. I am Marius Byron, master vampire, and I have *you* to thank for awakening me from my eternal slumber." His power pulsed through her, threatening to short circuit her brain.

"It wasn't intentional," Georgia rasped, "I'd have preferred you remain asleep."

His grip tightened painfully on her fingers before releasing her as he smiled.

"Erik warned me you had... spirit. That you would not bow down and simper at my feet." His accent was English, and Georgia couldn't fathom the world he had come from.

"Got that right." She swayed a little and put a hand to her eyes. Not only was her head throbbing, but her vision was also starting to darken at the edges. She yelped when hands gave her a light push backward, and, losing her balance, she toppled back into a chair that had suddenly appeared behind her.

"Sit before you fall down," Marius ordered.

He walked over to the fireplace and stood with his back to it, hands clasped loosely behind him, very much the gentleman of the manor. He watched her watching him.

"I have not yet decided what shall become of you, sweet Georgia. You and your dearly departed sister have given me back my life, and for that, I feel I owe you. But!" he held up a hand when she went to speak, "I can easily end your life in a heartbeat, snap your neck like a twig or simply drink you dry. Which is very tempting, my sweet Georgia, because your blood? Mmmmm, it is like ambrosia. I am keen to have more."

Suddenly he was in front of her, bending so he was looking directly into her eyes. The red in his gaze seemed to swirl and dip and send out a hypnotizing energy. She felt his energy pushing into her, and she cried out, the pain in her head amplifying. Blood trickled from her nose, and the room spun, black spots blurring her vision. Her stomach churned, and suddenly she vomited. Leaning forward in the chair, about to slide forward and faceplant into her own pile of vomit, a hand grabbed the back of her neck and held her in place.

"Erik! Heal her, clean her, make sure she is fed and rested. Then, I shall feed. I want this to last, and alas, in her present condition, I fear any more blood loss would be the end of her."

"Yes, Master." Erik dragged her from the chair, and she struggled to stay conscious as he dragged her into an enormous bathroom. She cringed when she caught sight of herself in the mirror. She was covered in dirt and filth, her hair matted and bloodstained, along with her clothes.

Erik slammed the door shut, and she heard a lock slide into place. He let her go and shoved her across the room while he turned and started to fill the bathtub. When he straightened, his evil eyes settled on her, and he stalked her across the room.

"I can hear your little heart beating so frantically," he drawled, obviously delighted at her panic. "What are you so scared of, Georgia? That I shall see you naked? That I shall have you? Or that I will drink your blood until your heart stops?"

She'd backed up against the counter, nowhere else to go, and could only watch helplessly as he approached.

In the blink of an eye, Erik brought the inside of his wrist up to his mouth and bit down before grabbing her and pressing the bleeding wound to her mouth. She jerked back in revulsion, clamping her lips shut.

"Drink!" he ordered, pulling her head back by her hair so sharply she cried out. As soon as her mouth opened, his blood trickled in. She tried to spit it out, but he kept his wrist pressed tightly against her mouth, squashing her lips back against her teeth. Eyes watering, she fought him, but she knew the blood was in her system. She could feel the tingling in her neck where her flesh was torn, knew it was knitting back together. The throbbing headache where she had hit her head was easing. He released her, and she spat at him, "Asshole."

He laughed. Grabbing her around the waist, he hauled her to the bath and dropped her in, clothes and all. The water was cold, making her gasp. She struggled against him, trying to get out, but he pressed a hand against her chest and forced her onto her back, fully submerging her under the water. She thrashed, panicking, fearing he would drown her.

He let her up, and she dragged in a shuddering breath, only to have him shove her under again. He repeated the process over and over again until she was exhausted, and her struggles ceased; she merely floated to the surface to grab a breath of air, no longer fighting him.

"That's more like it." He grinned. Finally relenting, he pulled her from the bath and stood looking at her as she shivered before him.

"Strip. You can do it yourself, or we can do it the fun way." He leered at her.

With trembling fingers, she worked her way out of her sodden clothing. Long mortifying moments later, she stood before him, skin pebbled with goosebumps and shivering. His eyes roamed over her naked body. She was helpless, naked, and trapped, and it infuriated her.

"Pervert."

He laughed, then he moved, and she couldn't help but flinch, but he merely opened the bathroom door, ushering her out. She was led back to her room in the basement. A mattress and blanket had been brought in, along with a tray of food. The door clanged shut behind her, locks sliding into place. On shaking legs, she sank down onto the mattress; pulling the blanket around her, she reached out for the food, hating that she needed to eat but knowing she needed to build up her strength if she had any chance of getting out of this alive.

CHAPTER
TWENTY

"Zak! Zak!" Frank's voice shouted at him, coming from a great distance. Frank's voice was urgent, insistent. What was it? Zak struggled to push through the darkness dragging him down. The blessed silence had been so peaceful, he'd wanted to stay, but then the noise had started to come back, and he knew in the back of his mind that there was something important he needed to be doing.

Rough arms were holding him, which strange. Why was Frank holding him? His eyes flickered open to look at his old friend.

"What's up?" he muttered.

Frank beamed at him, "Oh man! I thought you'd

247

bitten the big one." He indicated his bleeding wrist. "I had to force-feed you to try and get you to heal yourself. Never do that to me again." Awareness came back to him in a rush. Georgia had daggered him!

His hand went to his chest, his fingers brushing over the blood still wet on his skin and the tender spot where his wound was still healing. He looked at Frank.

"What happened?"

"You don't know?"

"Georgia?" Zak sat up, his eyes darting around the cave, searching for her.

"She's gone," Frank admitted gruffly. "I don't know what shit went down in here, but that original vamp *did* get awakened, drank Skye dry, and must've grabbed Georgia as a takeaway snack."

"*What?*" Zak surged to his feet, rushing over to examine the slab of rock that was now drizzled with fresh blood. The rock formation that had been there previously was gone. Even he hadn't realized that pile of fossilized stone had been an original vamp out for the count. His eyes landed on Skye's body, lying on the ground, her wrist a bloody mess.

"Oh, Skye," he murmured, crossing to her and

rolling her onto her back. Then he heard it. A very faint, ka-boom. Several long seconds later, another faint ka-boom.

"She's still alive!" he shouted. Frank appeared at his side, his brows drawn together in a frown.

"Oh my god. I thought she'd gone. Couldn't find a pulse. Can you save her?"

"I'll have to turn her. No other way to save her." Zak brought his own wrist up to his mouth when he froze. "Where's my ring?"

"What?"

"It's missing. Where is it? How did they get it off my finger?"

Frank frantically searched through the rubble. "You know," he grumbled, tossing rocks aside, "this means you must have truly died. For them to be able to take it from you."

"I know," Zak growled, thunder in his eyes.

"Can you turn her without the ring?"

"Yes. But her chances are much higher if I'm wearing it. The power of three angels behind me will go a long way to saving her. She doesn't have much time. Barely minutes."

Frank held up the ring in triumph. "Found it!"

Zak slid it back on his finger, feeling a rush of

energy pulse through him as he did so. The red river of blood still wound its way around the band. He'd wondered if the ring would no longer be active now that the original had been awakened, but it seems that was not the case.

He scored his wrist with his fangs and held it over Skye's mouth, his free hand holding her mouth open for the blood to drip in.

Ka-boom... ka-boom... ka... boom........... ka..... boom.........

Skye's heart stopped. Both men waited, praying Zak's blood had reached her in time. They weren't concerned with her heart stopping; it had to happen to transition into a vampire. They just hoped she'd gotten a couple of beats in to circulate Zak's blood. A minute stretched by, then two.

The two men looked at each other. They'd failed. Suddenly a mouth clamped onto Zak's wrist and began guzzling great greedy slurping sounds. Zak looked down at Skye with a grin, who had his arm in a death grip and was drinking deep from him.

"Welcome back."

Skye's eyes opened, and she looked at him, dazed. She dropped his arm in confusion.

"It's okay. Don't panic." He soothed her. Her

transition would start soon, and he needed to explain what was about to happen, or she would freak out big time.

Skye went to speak, but her voice failed her.

"Don't talk, listen. We don't have much time. You were dying. To save you, I had to turn you. Your transition will start soon, and I need to prepare you... and get you away from this place. I'm sorry, but it's going to hurt. Your body's molecular structure will change, and that is never a pleasant experience, but afterward? You're going to be stronger, faster, and more alive than you've ever felt before. When you awake after the transition, you're going to be thirsty for blood. I won't sugarcoat this for you because I need you to understand. Usually, these conversations are had before I turn someone, but you were turned in an emergency, so there was no time."

Skye watched and listened as Zak outlined what was going to happen. Her body would feel like it was on fire from the inside out. When that was over, she'd be in blood lust, a perilous time for a new vampire. But Zak had promised he'd be there to help her, and heaven help her she believed him.

She wasn't afraid. Okay, being a vampire hadn't been high on her wish list, but it was better than being dead. And the upshot? Maybe as a vampire, she'd have a better chance at saving her sister because she'd still been conscious when she'd seen Erik flip Georgia over his shoulder and disappear with her and the newly awakened original.

CHAPTER
TWENTY-ONE

It could have been hours; it could have been days. Georgia had no idea how much time had passed since Erik had left her locked in the basement.

Now that her head wasn't throbbing and her vision was no longer blurry, she could see the room better. Initially, she'd thought there were no windows, but now she could just make out a long narrow window at the top of the far wall that looked like it had been boarded up from the outside. The door was thick and solid. She'd given it a couple of shoulder thrusts, but it hadn't budged.

Her mind drifted to Skye, and her chest ached. Had she survived? Even though she knew it was unlikely, she clung to the hope. If anything, her sister was a fighter like she was. Praying for her sister to a God she rarely spoke to, she clasped her hands and closed her eyes. P*lease, Lord, just this one time?*

Then she thought of Zak, and tears filled her eyes. Her mind couldn't fathom that she wouldn't see him again, hear his voice, and feel his touch. They were only at the beginning, so how could they have reached the end so soon? And how could it have been Georgia herself who'd brought about the end? Why, for once in her life, hadn't she listened and just stayed put? But no, she was such a tough guy, always out to prove herself. *Yeah, job well done, loser*, she berated herself, *you couldn't manage to save your parents, and you couldn't save Zak. What use are you?*

She was lying on the mattress staring at the ceiling, wallowing in her misery, when the door suddenly flung open. She hadn't even heard approaching footsteps! Bloody vampires.

"Up!" Marius commanded.

Georgia slowly rose to her feet, eyeing him warily. She kept the blanket wrapped around her, hiding her body from view. Marius smirked but didn't comment. He simply ran his eyes over her.

Lightning-fast, his hand reached out and

snatched the blanket from her, the tug of the fabric being ripped away jerking her toward him. She caught herself before she touched him and danced backward before he could touch her.

Not fast enough. He was on her, his power smothering her mind and senses as his body crushed hers into the mattress. She could hear his laugh. Feel his hands pinning her down, the strength of him as he tore into her, the warm stickiness of her blood as it flowed from her torn neck.

She fought. She bucked, kicked, and twisted. Each movement tore her throat, yet she wouldn't lie docilely and let him feed on her. She wouldn't go down without a fight. She tried to bring a knee up to smash him in the groin, but he easily pinned her legs.

Her struggles slowed, the edge of her vision starting to fade. Finally, he lifted his head, those massive, grotesque fangs shimmering with her blood.

"Keep fighting. I love it. Just know this. Nobody is coming for you. No one." Then his weight was gone, and he was standing looking down at her. She couldn't move, her limbs heavy, her neck throbbing. She watched him with dull, glazed eyes, his presence pushing into her mind like a live wire across exposed nerve endings. Inside her head, she screamed and screamed and screamed.

That day set the standard for the following days. Daily feeding, daily torture. The days turned into weeks, weeks where she'd been kept his prisoner, and he'd reduced her to nothing.

Nobody is coming.

"Oh, Georgia, broken already?" He lay on her, his mouth at her traumatized neck. "You're mine now."

She floated in a haze of pain, heat, and horror. He could have healed her but didn't. He kept her weak, and to put an end to the pain and humiliation he'd reduced her to, she would have gladly taken her own life had she been able to.

The only relief? When he finally withdrew his fangs, and her mind was floating, up and away, somewhere else, away from here. During those moments, she was unaware. She was outside of herself, no pain, no fear. She'd slowly come back to awareness, broken and bleeding where he'd left her, a tray of food on the floor. She had no idea who brought it, never heard or saw them, but the food and water would appear each day. She forced herself to eat and drink and walk around and around in her cell, trying to keep up her strength.

No one else touched her. No one else saw her. Spoke to her. She was isolated and alone, and Marius was her world. Her world of never-ending agony. Thoughts of escape flitted through her mind, but so far, no solid plan. If an opportunity presented itself, she wouldn't hesitate. If it meant she was killed in the process, so be it. Death was more appealing than this.

Slowly a kernel of an idea came to her. The food tray. Whoever was bringing the food tray expected her to be comatose. They probably left the door open for those couple of minutes. That's all she needed, catch them off guard. She only had one shot at this.

During Marius's next visit, she stayed present. Tears streamed from her eyes at the pain of his bite, but she kept her mind present. His fingers bruised as they dug into her shoulders, and she almost let herself slip away. No! Stay! This was her chance; today was her chance. Marius was quiet, which helped. No taunting words or laughter, no groping at her body. He drank and moved away, not pausing to look down at her. He was distracted, and she was grateful, for she feared he would notice the change in her and sense something was up.

She was right! He strode to the door, flung it

open, and walked out, leaving it gaping open behind him. Straight away, a small form scurried in, carrying a tray. The person came closer, and Georgia realized it was a girl, a human. How odd. She'd have thought they'd have a vamp guarding her, but then she supposed they felt she was too weak to escape.

The girl was by her side, placing the tray on the floor. Now! Kicking out, she knocked the girl's feet from under her, sending her toppling backward. Springing up, she clamped a hand over the girl's mouth to stop any sound. The girl fought back, clearly no warrior by the way she ineffectively slapped at her. One punch to the jaw, and the girl was out like a light. No time. No time to steal the girl's clothes. No time, she had to make this quick.

Across the room, out the door, closing it behind her. Naked in the dim light of the hallway. Trembling legs carried her to the staircase, and she slowly crawled her way up them. Would they miss the girl? How long before someone came searching for her? She cracked open the door at the top of the stairs with shaking hands. Kitchen. Yes, that's right. She vaguely remembered when they'd first brought her here that the door to the basement was via the kitchen.

Empty. Bare feet made no sound across the tiled

floor; keeping low, she pressed against the cupboards, ears straining for any sound. She couldn't rely on her senses here. The house was full of vampires. She couldn't tell how close one was with all the signals jamming up her brain. She spied a sliding door. Darting across the room, she slid it open and silently slipped outside.

She'd done it! She was outside. It was pitch black, but her eyes were used to the dark now. She could make out the shape of trees not far away, so she broke into a run, streaking across what felt like lawn beneath her feet. Breath rasping, she clutched at the first tree, hugging the trunk and sliding her body around it, so she was hidden behind it. The bark scraped her skin, but she didn't feel it. Shouts sounded from the house. *Fuck!* Already?

Taking off at a run, she plowed through the trees, breath sawing in and out of aching lungs, twigs, and rocks digging into her bare feet as she raced through... what? A forest? Don't know, don't care, just keep running.

"Oooof," she was torpedoed from the side, a hard body diving into her, arms of steel trapping her arms by her side as they plowed into the dirt. She felt layers of skin ripping away where they landed. *No. No, no, no.* She screamed, kicked, bit, and scratched. A slap to the face had her seeing stars, and she was tossed over a shoulder, nausea roiling through her as the hard shoulder dug into her stomach.

In a matter of seconds, she was back in her cell, thrown painfully against the wall. Cuts and scrapes bled and stung, and only adrenaline was keeping her going. She couldn't have failed this. She couldn't. Yet she had. The proof was irrefutable.

Marius stormed into the cell, the door smashing back against the wall. His energy rolled from him in waves of anger as he stood before her.

Grabbing her by the throat, he spun her to face the wall. "Hold her." Her arms were stretched out from her sides, and a vamp on each side of her kept each wrist pinned against the wall. Then she heard it, a swish of air before the stinging ropes of a whip cut into the flesh of her back. Her breath hissed in, and she held it, unable to breathe, the pain in her back stunning her. On it went, lash after lash. She didn't scream, couldn't, she had no breath. She was dying.

She didn't remember it stopping, but it must have. She was lying on the mattress, her bloody back pressing against the foam, the pressure of her own weight adding to the torture.

"If you think I'll kill you and let you escape me like that, you're sorely mistaken."

She couldn't focus; she could see a dark shape standing over her, but everything was shimmering and moving, the walls swaying, the floor moving up and down like she was at sea.

"There is no escape, Georgia. You're mine. And no one is coming."

No one is coming.

He'd said that before, but she'd still hoped there was a chance of rescue. That Frank and the other warriors would try and find her. They hadn't. Marius was right. No one was coming. At that moment, she willed her heart to stop. Just stop beating. This could all be over. Stop damn you. But it didn't. It kept on, ka-thump, ka-thump, ka-thump. She closed her eyes on a shudder.

Dark mist swirled, wrapping around her, bringing that oh so old and familiar tingling. She almost grinned. It seemed so long ago when Zak had invaded her dreams. Oh, how she missed him. Her imagination was playing tricks on her, fooling her into thinking he was with her, but she'd take it. She'd take any comfort she could in this hellhole.

"Mine." His voice rolled through her mind, so familiar. He'd said it before, hadn't he? Yes. She was his. At the time, she'd denied it, but now? Yes. His. Marius was fooling himself if he thought Georgia was really his—she would always belong to Zak. Always.

"Georgia... love... I'm coming for you."

"Nobody is coming," she whispered. She felt those warm lips against her forehead, so light, so gentle, careful not to hurt her.

"I'm coming. Hold on."

"Okay." She thought she felt him grin at her uncharacteristic compliance, but it hurt too much to try and figure things out. With a ragged sigh, she slipped into oblivion.

CHAPTER
TWENTY-TWO

"She's alive," Zak addressed his warriors in the conference room. "Barely."

"You reached her?" Skye jumped to her feet in excitement. "What did she say? Where is she?"

"We didn't get the chance to chat. She's weak. Hurt. Barely conscious."

"Can you find her? Lock onto her or something?"

Zak sighed, pinching the top of his nose between his fingers. "Last time, it was easy because of the first blade, but she doesn't have it with her, so now it's more difficult. I will keep trying, but at least we know she's alive. And she knows we're coming for her."

"Sire!" Aston spun from the console where he'd

been tapping away, "Veronica is on the move. Big time!"

Frank and Zak gathered behind Aston to watch on the screen as the tracking device they'd hidden on Veronica flashed, moving across the screen, jumping from spot to spot, hundreds of miles between each landing.

"What the?" Frank muttered.

"She's teleporting," Zak muttered. "She doesn't have the skill or power, so someone is jumping with her."

"Who?"

"My best guess? The original that they've woken. I've known of no other who can teleport."

"Looks like they've stopped." Anton pointed to the now stationary red dot blinking on the screen.

"Where?"

"Azur Falls. Give me a minute, I can zoom in and get you an exact address."

"Perfect. Frank, round up the troops. We're going to Azur Falls."

"And Skye?"

"Shit. She's too new. Ok, someone is going to have to stay behind with her."

"Dainton will do it. He's a little bit smitten with her; he's been spending an awful lot of time with her already, showing her the ropes, so to speak."

"See to it," Zak ordered, his mind already miles away. "Aston, arrange a private charter. We're going to have to fly in. I won't be able to teleport since I have no reference point. We can't fly commercial; we'll need our weapons. Arrange transport the other end as well."

"On it."

IT WAS hard to count the passing of time when you had no clock to watch, no window to mark the passage of time between night and day. Georgia lay on the mattress and dozed. Her whole body was a giant ball of pain. She sat up, the dried blood on her back stuck to the mattress, reopening the wounds when she gritted her teeth and pulled herself upright.

The food tray was there, waiting for her. She ate and drank, then looked at the door. Something looked different. Tilting her head, she studied it. It looked...bowed. Twisted. Had Marius damaged it in his rage?

Hobbling over, she took a closer look, running

her fingers around the edge where the wood was now warped. With an excited breath, she realized she could squeeze her fingers through the gap. If she could push the deadbolt in... she'd be free. Again. She knew if she chanced a second attempt and was caught, Marius would most likely kill her. Even though he said he wouldn't, she knew he couldn't tolerate disobedience. She'd tried to flee from him twice. She was pretty sure that was an act punishable by death. Bring it on, she thought with a grin.

Sweating, trembling, fingers bleeding, she did it. The lock clicked in. She froze. Could she do this? Could she try to escape again, even weaker than before, risk her life, for Marius surely would kill her this time, for one last shot at freedom? Hell yeah!

Her dream of Zak flickered through her mind, giving her strength.

Her luck held. No one was outside the door, guarding her. Moving up the stairs on silent feet, she eased open the door at the top, cautiously peeking beyond into the kitchen. No one was in sight, and a quick glance to the right had her sighing in relief. Sunlight streamed in through the kitchen window.

No sneaking this time; she quickly hurried to the sliding door and let herself outside.

The sunlight hurt her eyes after weeks of being kept in the dark. She squinted and raised an arm to shelter her face as she took stock of her surroundings. It was hot, the air heavy and oppressing. Vamps wouldn't last a minute in this blazing sun.

The house was as huge as she'd imagined. It was at least three stories high, with carefully manicured gardens. To the right of her was a massive garage. Keeping low, she darted across and tried the side door. Locked. Glancing down the driveway, she saw that it was barred by massive gates and security cameras atop them. No going out the front way.

To the left was the crop of trees where she'd been re-captured. Should she go that way? Who knew what was beyond those trees; she just knew she needed to put as much space as possible between her and the house.

Following the length of the garage, she inched along towards the rear of the property. The garden was huge. The area directly behind the house had a lush green lawn surrounded by well-cared-for flower beds around the perimeter. A hedge divided a swimming pool from view of the house and another hedge beyond that.

She skirted around the pool, breathing easier

now she was out of view of the house. Behind the second hedge was a small shed that looked like it housed the pump and materials for the pool. Alongside were gardening implements, rubble, old building scraps, and an old timber fence running across what she assumed was the property's boundary.

She scrambled over the fence, dropping with a thud and a wheeze into the alley beyond. Keeping to the shade as best she could, she limped along, stones digging into her bare feet, sweat running into her eyes. She cast a look upward, the sun beating down from directly overhead. Midday. That didn't give her long to get far, far away. As soon as they realized she was missing, they'd be out looking for her in force, and with their sense of smell and tracking skills, holing up somewhere nearby was not an option.

She'd been on the move for over an hour following the crude dirt track. She must be getting closer to civilization as other houses began to appear, backing onto the alley. She had no idea where she was, but these alleys were old; under her feet, the dirt had changed to cobblestones, most of them covered by a thin layer of soil. No one had bothered to lay bitumen, yet the glimpses she got of houses on the other side of the fences showed well-kept expensive-looking homes.

Spying women's clothes on a washing line in someone's backyard, she stopped to peer through a gap in the fence, checking no one was in the garden, and there was no guard dog to greet her. Her luck held, and she hauled herself up and over the fence, dashing to the back of the house before she could be spotted.

After several minutes of absolutely nothing happening, she braved moving up the back stairs and onto the veranda that ran the length of a cottage. Peeking carefully through the windows, she watched for signs of movement. It looked like no one was home. She figured that if this was a weekday, the owners were most likely at work. She looked around the garden again. No sign of toys or children's play equipment supported her theory that whoever lived here was out for the day, most likely at work.

Perfect.

Several potted plants sat on the veranda, and she lifted all of them, searching for a spare key. She reached above the door and searched along the sill, but still no luck. *Come on,* she fumed. *Everyone has a spare key hidden somewhere.* Back down the stairs to the flower bed off to the side. There! Rocks. Sure enough, one of them was fake, and beneath it? A hidden compartment containing a spare key. *Eureka*.

Letting herself in, she flipped the lock behind her. She felt a twinge of regret at breaking into a stranger's home, but it was survival; she wasn't there to pilfer their TV and stereo to sell on the black market. Although looking at the modern furnishings and expensive equipment, it would fetch a pretty penny.

A wave of dizziness washed over her, and she sunk to the floor, putting her head between her knees and drawing deep breaths. It was hot in the house, and she was even hotter; her unprotected skin had started to burn. Her wounds hurt, and she desperately wanted to lie down and rest. The tiles beneath her were cool, and she was tempted to stretch out on them. Gritting her teeth, she forced herself back to her feet; staggering to the sink, she turned on the tap and stuck her mouth under the flowing water, drinking thirstily. Better.

She found the master bedroom and checked out the walk-in robe. Male and female clothing hung neatly. Perfect. She needed clothes; it had been pure luck that no one had spotted her limping naked along the alley. Stepping into the ensuite, she froze when she caught sight of herself in the mirror above the vanity.

She was covered in dirt, bruises, and dried blood. Her hair was a tangled mess. Leaning toward the mirror, she moved her hair away from her neck to examine the damage Marius had wreaked on her. It was bad. Her skin was a bloody and torn mess from beneath her ear all the way to her collarbone. Twisting as best she could, she took a look at her stinging back. A dozen whip marks marred her skin, crisscrossing her back from shoulder to hip. They weren't deep, just deep enough to bleed and hurt like crazy.

Turning on the shower, she got the water to the perfect temperature before holding her breath and stepping beneath the spray. This was going to sting. She was right. As the water hit her open wounds, her breath hissed out between clenched teeth; she forced herself to stay under the spray until it became bearable.

Quickly she cleaned herself, washed her hair, and then stepped out, wrapping a towel around herself. Blood was oozing from her neck and from a couple of the lashes on her back. Nothing she could do about her back; she couldn't reach it, but she rummaged in the vanity for a first aid kit and placed a large dressing over the oozing hole in her neck as best she could.

Now that the dirt, grime, and blood were washed away, she could see the bruises all over her. Her tan had faded, and the continual blood loss had leached any remaining color from her, leaving her with an unhealthy pallor.

Back in the bedroom, she searched a dresser, pulling out a pair of women's black yoga pants and a matching t-shirt. She found a pair of flip flops that were only a size too big and shoved her feet into them, then grabbed what appeared to be a gym bag from the wardrobe, dumping the contents onto the floor.

Some loose change fell out, and she snatched it up, then quickly rifled through the clothes hanging in the closet, searching pockets for forgotten notes hastily shoved into pockets on a night out. *Bingo*. A twenty in a suit pocket and another twenty in one of the evening bags hanging from a hook.

Back in the kitchen, she grabbed what food she could: a couple of apples, some energy bars, and a couple of bottles of water from the fridge. She shoved them into the duffel bag and swung it over her shoulder before letting herself out the front door.

She'd been at the house for almost an hour, and the sun was starting to dip in the sky. She needed to get further away. Walking as fast as she could in her weakened condition, she followed the street, praying she'd find a bus stop or some sort of public transport soon. Luck was with her, ten minutes later she saw a sign to a train station. Even better.

She boarded the first train that arrived, paid for her ticket, and took a seat with a shaky breath. She leaned forward, resting her forearms on her knees to keep her tender back from sticking to the back of the seat. Thankfully her borrowed t-shirt was black and would hide any blood that seeped through.

She allowed herself to relax a little, safe in the knowledge that she was moving further away from the enemy, and it was going to be harder for them to track her now she was on a train. She ate an apple and sipped on her water throughout the journey, then dozed, the sway of the carriage and click-clack of the tracks soothing.

Eventually, the train reached its final destination. Azur Falls. How on earth she'd gotten to Azur Falls, she didn't know, and she'd never been here before, but at least she was in the same country. Following the crowd off the train, she allowed herself to get swept up in the rush, bursting forth onto what appeared to be the main street. Then the crowd scattered, heading off in all directions.

Taking a minute to get her bearings, Georgia headed towards the center of town. Fatigue pulled at her; now that she was out of the coolness of the train, the heat and humidity covered her like a wet blanket, making it difficult to move with any sense of urgency. She just wanted to sleep.

The vision of a payphone a hundred meters away snapped her out of it like a bucket of cold water. Rushing to the phone, she dropped the duffel bag at her feet and rummaged around for coins. Heart hammering in her chest, she lifted the receiver and fed in some of the cash she'd taken from the cottage. She dialed Skye's cell number, the only one (besides her own) that she had memorized.

It rang, then went to voicemail. Just hearing her sister's voice brought tears to her eyes.

"Skye? Skye, it's Georgia." Her voice broke, and she wiped a hand across her wet eyes, sniffing, "Please be alive. Please. Ummm. I'm in a shitload of trouble here. I'm in Azur Falls—don't ask, I have no clue. But I've no phone, no money and I don't know what my plan is, so you can't call me back. I'll try and call again later... okay? Please be okay. I love you."

The sun was now hovering low on the horizon, not long until sunset. Shit, she needed to get off the streets and spend the night somewhere safe. But where? She didn't have enough money for a hotel room, and sleeping on the streets wasn't an option. Not only would there be vamps out there looking for her, but the usual street thugs as well, and she wasn't strong enough to fight anyone off.

She sat for a moment as she pondered her next move. She had food and water. She just needed safe shelter.

Then it hit her. A church! Vampires couldn't enter holy ground. Could they? She'd take the chance since it was the only idea she'd been able to come up with. And wouldn't you know it, from where she was sitting, in the distance, she could see a cross sitting high above the rooftops. A church.

Swinging her duffel back onto her shoulder, she took off as fast as she could manage; the sun was going down fast. She wasn't sure if it had to be completely dark before vampires could be out, but she also needed to get to the church before they locked the doors. That's if she wasn't too late already.

Everything feels like it takes forever when you're on foot, she grumbled, finally trudging up the street to the church. Thankfully the lights of the church were on as twilight settled across the city.

The double doors stood open and welcoming, and she breathed a sigh of relief as she stepped across the threshold, hot and exhausted.

A few people were inside praying. A priest was at the altar, laying out what he needed for his next service. Georgia crossed herself and slid into a pew at the back. Since she was there, she threw up a prayer for Skye, that she was alive and recovering, and for Zak, that he was at peace and that she loved him. She hadn't really realized that she loved him when they were together, but over the last couple of horrendous weeks, she'd known what was in her heart. A tear slid down her cheek that she'd never had the chance to tell him.

She sat quietly in reflection, her body slowly cooling down after the rush to get there, her breath settling into an easy rhythm. People began to file into the church, obviously preparing for an evening service. She sat and listened, pondering the age-old question, is there life after death? The priest seemed to think so.

The service went for an hour, then people began

to leave again, many stopping to chat with the priest. Georgia slid farther along the pew toward the wall. At the end, there was a two-foot gap between the wall and where the pew ended, enough space for her to hunker down and not be seen unless the priest decided to walk along that side of the church. Still, she'd been watching him carefully, and he'd never veered off the center walkway. She crouched down and waited.

Once the lights were out, the doors were locked, and the priest was gone, Georgia stretched out under the pew, using the duffel as a pillow, and closed her eyes, for the first night in weeks feeling relatively safe. Maybe she'd dream of Zak again. A soft smile curved her lips as slumber claimed her.

TWENTY-THREE

"C'mon Dainton, ring him again!" Skye was practically jumping up and down in agitation.

"I've left him a message to call me as soon as he lands. He will. There's no point leaving him a dozen messages." Dainton looked over at her and sighed, taking both of her hands in his. "He'll find her, don't worry."

"I can't believe I missed her call!" Skye sobbed, face crumbling. "After all these weeks of nothing, not knowing if she was alive or dead, I missed her damn call!"

"You heard her; she'll call back when she can. She's smart. And tough. She's survived this long," he soothed, pulling her against his chest and running a calming hand up and down her back.

Minutes passed in silence before Skye raised her head, her eyes bleeding red.

"Hungry?" Dainton guessed, reaching over to the cooler and pulling out a bag of blood.

"Hungry. Again." She took the bag from him and roughly pushed her fangs into it, draining it dry within minutes.

Dainton's phone buzzed, and he snatched it up before Skye could get to it.

"Boss," he greeted.

"News?" Zak asked.

"Georgia rang Skye's mobile. We missed the call, but she left a voice message. She's alive."

There was a moment's silence, then Zak barked, "Do we know where she is?"

"Azur Falls. That's all we've got."

"Well isn't that handy? Just so happens we're in Azur Falls too."

"It's looking more and more like Veronica is mixed up in this, doesn't it?" Dainton asked sadly.

"It's sure looking that way. Look, I'm going to put Aston on. He can give you instructions on tracing Georgia's call."

Zak paced impatiently while Aston and Dainton

talked. Zak could feel Skye's emotions through their bond, now that she was sired to him. She was swinging from absolute exultation to anger and frustration. He sympathized with how she felt. Knowing for sure that Georgia was alive and not being able to go to her straight away was killing him.

Aston hung up the phone and turned to him. "Okay, traced it to a public phone outside the supermarket in the town center. I reckon we go there and pick up her scent we'll be able to track her."

"Good man." Zak slapped him on the back.

Piling into the hired SUV, they sped from the airport, unconcerned with tolls and speeding tickets. Such menial matters took a back seat when it came to finding Georgia.

It was nearing midnight when Zak and his warriors approached the public phone Georgia had made the call from.

"Not picking up on any vamps," Cole muttered, scanning the area intently. "You?"

"Nah." Kyan and Heath replied in unison.

"Spread out. And keep an eye out. If she was here, they're bound to be looking for her. Luck is on our side that we got here first, but that's not to say

they haven't picked up her trail somewhere else."
Frank commanded.

Zak strode up to the phone and picked up the receiver. Others had used the phone after Georgia, but taking a deep breath, he picked up her scent. It was faint, masked with another smell over the top. Clever girl, wearing someone else's clothes. He smiled.

"She was definitely here. Let's go." He followed her trail, stopping every now and then to breathe air deep into his lungs, his senses picking up her unique signature and guiding the way. They turned into the street and eyed the church on top of the hill.

"Fuckin' clever girl." Frank grinned.

"She is," Zak agreed, returning the smile. "You lot fan out around the church, keep a close eye out but don't let yourselves be seen. We don't want to give away her location."

They flew up the street, disappearing into the shadows as Zak walked up the steps of the church. He tested the doors. Locked. With a shrug, he stepped up to a window and peered into the church before transporting himself inside. Being half-angel had its perks... being able to walk unhindered into a church had never come in handy before, but right now? A godsend.

The church was dark and quiet, but if he listened closely, he could hear soft, even breathing. Following the sound, he walked along the pew and crouched, looking beneath it. There she lay, palms pressed together with her cheek resting on them, legs curled up, sound asleep.

His breath left him in a rush, and he let his head sag. She was alive. She was safe. He let it sink in a minute before reaching out to stroke her cheek.

She awoke with a start, slamming her head into the pew above her.

"Ow. Fuck!" she yelped, then realized where she was and what she was running from. She scrambled backward on the wooden floorboards, pissed that she'd been discovered.

"Georgia? It's me."

She froze. Was that? "Zak?"

"Yeah. Zak." He smiled, his teeth shining white in the darkness. She was in his arms before he could blink, knocking him off balance and onto his backside. He laughed, wrapping his arms around her and holding on.

"Oh god, oh god, oh god," she cried, pulling back to run her hands over his face and chest and back again, "you're really here. You're not dead? Oh god, I thought you were dead." Sobs tore from her chest, heart-wrenching cries that tore him apart.

"Sssh, it's ok. I'm here. I'm not dead. It's all ok," he soothed, rocking her in his arms and dropping kisses on the top of her head. Finally, she calmed, sniffing and wiping at her wet face.

"How? I was sure I'd killed you." At her own words, she started to cry again, "I'm so sorry. So sorry. I didn't mean to. I was aiming for Erik, and he moved, and suddenly you were in front of me, and the knife just went... into... your... chest..."

"Hey. I'm here. I'm okay. I survived. It's not your fault. I know you didn't mean it." He cradled her face in his palms and wiped away her tears with his thumbs.

"I love you," she whispered, her drowning eyes meeting his.

"I love you too. So very much," he whispered in return, dropping his mouth to hers and kissing her so, so softly. Gently he pulled away.

"As much as I'd like to continue this right here, we should leave."

She nodded, allowing him to help her to her feet. She grabbed the duffel and slung it over her shoulder.

"Are Marius and his goons here?" she asked, clasping his hand.

"Who's Marius?" Zak asked.

"The vampire who took me," she bit out, looking around with a wild glint in her eye. "The grand master poo-bar."

"Not yet. We couldn't sense them when we picked up your trail, which is why we need to get moving now before they catch up."

He teleported them outside and called his team around him. They stood in a group hug, and he teleported them all back to Redmeadows.

"Georgia!" Skye squealed, flying across the room and crashing into her sister with such force she threw them both across the room. They landed with a crash, Georgia landing painfully on the floor with a groan, Skye on top of her.

"Skye?" she whispered, eyeing her sister, who was smiling back at her... with fangs... and eyes that were starting to glow red.

"I'm... so... glad... you're alive." Skye clearly struggled to get the words out. Squeezing her eyes closed and then opening them again, "Damn, you smell so good," she breathed, leaning forward, fangs extended, and aimed for Georgia's neck.

Dainton flew in from the side, tackling Skye with

a powerful body blow that sent them both crashing into the far wall.

"Bloodlust," Frank commented.

"Yup," Dainton agreed, pulling Skye to her feet and hustling her out the door away from her human sister.

Georgia lay dazed on the floor. Skye was a vampire? She hadn't even thought of that as a possibility in all her prayers that her sister be saved. Guess she should've.

"Are you ok? Are you hurt?" Zak appeared above her, frowning in concern. She'd taken a hell of hard landing when Skye had launched herself at her.

"I'm really tired," Georgia admitted, letting her eyes drift closed for just a minute. Her back was screaming in agony, the rough landing making her wounds bleed. Again. Her eyes fluttered open again when she heard Zak's hissed breath. "What?"

He was looking at her neck, at the blood that was seeping through the dressing she'd applied earlier.

"I'm sorry," she whispered.

He looked at her incredulously, "What on earth are you sorry for? He did this to you!"

"It's all my fault. None of this would have happened if I'd stayed put in the first place. Like you told me to. I followed you into the mine, I brought the dagger in, I triggered all of these events." Silent tears ran from the corners of her eyes and soaked into her hair.

Zak pulled her into a sitting position and wiped her face. She winced, her shirt sticking to her back.

"It's not your fault. The wheels had been set in motion long before you got involved. Eons ago. Sometimes fate just has to play the part she was dealt, and as much as we rant about it, cry over it, blame ourselves over it, really, we have no control. It was meant to happen; all we can do is salvage what we can."

He paused, sniffing the air. His eyes landed on her neck and the dressing that was slowly leaking blood. He took a deeper breath, eyes narrowed. Hauling her to her feet, he spun her until she faced away from him. He didn't touch her, but she could practically feel his eyes exploring every inch of her.

"Your back... is bleeding," he growled.

"Most likely." She shrugged, trying to play down the extent of her injuries.

"All over. It looks like you're bleeding... all over." He snarled, and she shrieked when the fabric was suddenly torn from her back.

Hisses echoed as the warriors behind him

caught sight of her torn skin from the whipping. The silence that filled the room was thick and heavy.

"Jesus fucking Christ," Anton swore.

"He will fucking pay for this," from Cole.

"Bastard," Heath cursed.

"This is war," Kyan said.

Georgia started to tremble, clutching her torn shirt to her chest. She was so glad to be back with these guys, to feel their outrage over her treatment, but suddenly it was overwhelming. Every breath hurt, every drop of blood she lost was one drop she couldn't afford to lose, and when she remembered that she thought they weren't coming for her, that nobody was coming, she broke. Great sobs tore through her, dragged from her very soul.

Zak swept her into his arms and carried her upstairs to his room. He laid her on his bed, his voice soothing as he murmured comforting words to her.

"You put the bed together," she murmured, looking pleased.

"I did. I had to have you near me, and this seemed the best way." He brushed his hand across her brow, chasing away the headache that was starting to pound behind her eyes.

"You need to be healed," he began, his voice low, "it's going to be rough."

"Couldn't be worse," she whispered, not meeting his eyes.

He laid his palm over each lash on her back as gently as he could. The first white-hot sting she bit her lip and remained rigid on the bed; breath held until she thought her lungs were on fire. There was no reprieve; he had to keep going, and she had so many cuts across the length of her back. She cried out, trying to twist away.

"I'm sorry, I'm sorry... it'll be over soon, love, shhh..." Zak healed her back as quickly as possible, closing his ears to her screams.

Finally, he was finished. Her skin was once again perfect, unmarred by the vicious whip marks. But Georgia was undone. Trembling, shivering, and shaking, making funny noises in her throat. He rolled her over, untangling her from the torn remains of the t-shirt that she had clutched in her hands. Her eyes were closed, the dark lashes stark against her white skin.

Zak held her and rocked her, and soothed her while seething inside. Marius and Erik would pay for what they had done. Their lives were forfeit; he didn't care what it took. He'd see to it.

She groaned in his arms, eyes fluttering open.

"I'm so, so sorry." Zak's voice, raw and broken.

"S'ok," she murmured, "fixing me."

His eyes dropped to her neck. He was worried it would scar, and he didn't want the marks that would be a constant reminder to both of them. This would need more than just his energy.

"Sweetheart?"

She roused again, looking at him.

"I need to take care of your neck."

"K."

"We need to try something different."

"K."

"Sweetheart, open your eyes, look at me."

Struggling, she dragged her lids open and locked onto his face.

"Your neck is in really bad shape. I don't want to hurt you anymore. I can't. So we're going to do this another way."

"'Nother way?" she slurred, eyes squinting, trying to focus on him.

"Mmmm. C'mon." He pulled her up to lean back against his chest, where he was propped against the headboard. Then his wrist was at her lips, pressing something wet against them. She flicked out her tongue and tasted blood. Her body tensed, but he soothed her, his free hand stroking up and down her arm as he coaxed her into taking more.

Already exhausted, she had no energy to fight him or argue with him. He brought his wrist up to her mouth again and coaxed her to open, to suck, to take his blood into herself. She tried, the coppery flavor foreign to her. Honestly, she couldn't see the appeal. Who'd want to be a vampire? Then the effects hit her; the torn muscles and flesh in her neck started to move, re-align, and the pain was excruciating. She pushed Zak's arms away and yelled, her body practically convulsing.

While his blood went to work healing her, Zak laid his hand over her neck and sent his energy into her as well, a double-pronged attack. He soothed, he kissed, he murmured nonsensical words while she panted against him, skin sheened in sweat. Her head lolled, heavy against him when she passed out. He thought it better this way, hating himself for bringing her more pain even though he was healing her.

It hurt him to see her so broken, his ballsy, brave Georgia, who didn't take shit from anyone.

Zak pushed as much healing energy into her as he could while she was out cold. Her wounds were worse than she realized, deep and containing the venom of a master vampire.

He eased out from under her, laying her flat on

the bed. With gentle hands, he stripped her, healing the scrapes he found on her legs and the cuts on the bottom of her feet. He noticed her skin's paleness and weight loss, how her hip bones were jutting sharply, and her rib cage and collarbone starkly apparent. Once satisfied he'd healed every single one of her injuries, he tucked her beneath the covers, crawling in next to her and cradling her in his arms as she slept.

TWENTY-FOUR

"She has what?" Marius's yell bounced off the walls. Erik shuffled in place, angry that Georgia had gotten away; his own feelings on the matter, however, were nothing compared to the rage emanating from Marius.

"Escaped, my Lord."

"How did this happen?" face inches from Erik's, he seethed.

"We do not know, my Lord. Her door remains locked."

Erik's eyes bulged as Marius plunged a hand into his chest, fingers wrapped around his heart.

"Find her and destroy her." Marius pulled his hand from Erik's chest, flinging blood across the floor.

Without a word, Erik spun on his heel and stalked from the room, his own fury radiating out from him in waves. She was meant to be his. When Marius tired of her, she had been promised to *him*. He'd waited long enough, and now she'd escaped. Again. Only this time, she'd gotten away. He would rip her fucking throat out, no matter how sweet her blood tasted or how much he craved her body. She was finished.

"Marius," a soft feminine voice chided. Marius turned his gaze to Veronica, lounging on an antique love seat.

"What?" he snapped, clearly annoyed at having a human, a *human*, slip through his clutches. Never in his millennia of a lifetime had this happened.

"Calm, my love," she crooned, slowly rising and seductively moving across the room to him. Her pale hands cupped his face. "I can help. I know where the girl will be. And I bet I know how she got out," she purred, rubbing herself along the front of him. She smirked in satisfaction when she felt his erection surge against her and his hands clamp down hard on her waist.

"Tell me."

"Zak, my sire. He can teleport. And he can dream walk. He could easily have teleported her out of there. He would have taken her back to his home in Redmeadows."

"Erik informed me Zak was killed in the cavern."

"I don't know about that." Veronica shrugged. "But I do know that I can still feel the sire bond, and that wouldn't be the case if he was dead."

"True. So the bond has not been severed?"

"No."

"Then it is long overdue." Marius began to pull away from her, but she stayed him with a hand on his chest.

"Before you go rushing off, I have a better idea. Zak will be expecting you to retaliate, yes?"

"Of course."

"And he'll be expecting you straight away."

"Naturally."

"I say, let him wait. I know him, and it'll drive him nuts not knowing what your plans are, why you haven't turned up breathing fire on his doorstep. Instead, let's have a little fun here first. You. Me. A couple of blood slaves."

Marius threw back his head and laughed before planting a kiss on Veronica's blood-red lips.

"Oh, you minx! I like the way you think. Tell me all about your sire. There is clearly more to him than meets the eye. But first..." He pushed her to her knees in front of him, and she obligingly unzipped his trousers, his erection springing free. With no hesitation, she took him into her mouth, no complaints when he grabbed her hair and thrust into her until he climaxed.

"Zak, c'mon, it's been three days. I'm fine, I swear!" Georgia chided the overprotective vampire slash angel standing in front of her.

"You are still too pale," he growled.

"That'll change once I get some sun. If I'm kept indoors all the time, then yes, I'm going to be pale. I don't get it. You can come with me; the sun doesn't affect you. What's the problem?"

"The problem is I'd feel better if my warriors were there to protect you. You know if you return to your workshop during daylight that they cannot."

"I doubt he'll bother with me," Georgia shrugged, "he was planning on killing me anyway. I don't think he'll bother coming this far to exact his revenge. Oh, I'm sure they searched for me at the time, but I seriously doubt they would bother themselves with me."

"Don't kid yourself. Marius did not let you go.

You escaped. That is the equivalent of a slap to the face. And you do not get to slap a master vampire in the face and live to talk about it."

"Well, why hasn't he come already? If he's hell-bent on revenge?"

"Because he knows exactly where you are. Erik knows where you live, knows about your relationship with Skye, and that you would never leave her. I'm sure the grapevine has filled them in that Skye has been turned. And I'm sure he now knows all about me."

"You? How?"

"Veronica is with him. Her tracker is still active. I know exactly where he is... why do you think I was in Azur Falls? I was on my way to the mansion he'd commandeered when the call came in about you."

"Sorry, my timing was pretty poor, eh?"

"Your timing was perfect. I was hunting him down to find you." Zak pulled her into his arms. "I was going to find you. It was too coincidental that Veronica was suddenly in Azur Falls. But then you managed to save yourself and lead me right to you." He kissed the top of her head.

Georgia sighed against him, "I'm really sick of all this Veronica and Marius talk," she confessed, wrapping her arms around his waist.

"It's not going to go away; we're going to need to be ready for when he strikes," Zak murmured, distracted by the feel of her pressed up against him, her hands roaming across his lower back then dropping to squeeze his butt.

"We should train again," Georgia purred, rubbing her pelvis against his hardness.

"You call this training?" he chuckled, sliding a hand around the back of her neck and tilting her face up to him. Dropping kisses across her face, "We've been 'training' every night since you got home."

"Practice makes perfect," she captured his mouth with hers, dueling her tongue with his and sliding it erotically across his teeth. Zak lifted her, wrapping her legs around his waist he leaned them against the wall, the kiss spinning them both out of control.

"The boys?" she breathed, writhing against him.

"They won't come in," he assured her. With a pulse of energy, he shoved the conference room door shut. His men weren't stupid, and they'd learned over the last three days that he and Georgia could be found anywhere on the property enjoying each other's bodies. Georgia had no idea how often they'd been 'busted,' and the sheepish vampires had hastily retreated. Now they approached with caution, making sure Zak was 'decent' for company before entering any room.

"The table," Georgia gasped, arching her neck as Zak nibbled his way from her ear down.

"Perfect," he agreed, stripping her of her clothes and following the path his hands had made with his mouth and tongue. When her knees threatened to give out, he spun her and bent her over the table. She gasped when her breasts flattened against the cold surface, her gasp soon turning to a groan when she felt the weight of him at her back and his mouth sucking the back of her neck. He hadn't drunk from her since her return. In fact, there had been no fang play at all, and she missed it.

"Bite me," she whispered, longing to feel that rush of lust that only his bite could deliver, all thoughts of Marius's painful bite disappearing from her mind.

"No." Instead, he nibbled his way down her spine to her luscious rear, gently nipping her rounded cheek but refusing to bite.

"Please," she begged, her breath hitching in her throat when his fingers moved between her legs, spreading her thighs and moving his body between them. She could feel the hard length of him at her entrance and pushed back. He chuckled and denied her, teasing her with strokes but no penetration.

She struggled to sit up, but he forced her back down with a hand in the middle of her back.

"Bite me, you fucker," she cursed, wriggling against him. He laughed again and lowered his torso along her back as he slid his length into her, her hot, wet tightness squeezing him.

"Mmmmmmm."

"Couldn't have said it better," he murmured in her ear, rocking his hips as he slid in and out in gentle strokes. She pushed back with each stroke, and he reveled in the feel of her, her scent, her warmth.

"Zak," she practically sobbed. He stilled. She sounded distressed.

"Have I hurt you?" he asked, brows furrowing in concern.

"No. I need more Zak." Her breath hitched, "I remember your bite, how exquisite it feels, then Marius desecrated that memory. I need new memories, Zak... please."

He pushed into her again, leaning on his arms and pounding hard. She groaned beneath him, and he could feel her nearing orgasm. Pushing her hair away from the back of her neck, he kept up the unrelenting pace, bending and sinking his teeth into the nape of her neck. She shattered beneath him, her muscles tightening around him and milking him until he joined her, the sweetness of her blood clouding his mind and her body draining him dry.

"Oh, God." She shuddered, finally stirring. He'd collapsed on top of her and, for a moment, had forgotten that he was probably crushing her.

"Are you ok?"

"I'm more than ok. I'm perfect," she purred, wriggling to turn in his arms, so she was facing him. One cheek was pink where she'd laid her face against the table surface, and the friction of his pounding into her had bruised the soft skin. He cupped her cheek and sent out a healing pulse, the pinkness soon settling.

She grinned as he stood before her, her legs wrapped around him, the rest of her body laid out on the table.

"I like this position," she commented idly.

"You do?" He was hard again and entered what she had laid out so enticingly before him with no preamble.

"Oh yes." She propped herself up on her elbows and watched where their bodies joined. He looked down and had to admit it was a pretty good view.

Her wetness glistened on his skin as he withdrew, then pushed back inside of her, her body automatically adjusting to accommodate him. His thumb gently massaged her, and he watched in fascination as her body arched, her elbows collapsing as she lay flat on her back, her hips jerking in response to the brush of his thumb against the most sensitive part of her.

He continued the erotic massage while surging into her. Unable to take it anymore, he leaned over her, hands planted on either side of her head as his hips hammered against her. The change of position had him rubbing deliciously against her; he was everywhere, in and around her, and she was overwhelmed. Her orgasm hit her in a wave, spinning her out of control and splintering into a million pieces. Two more thrusts, and he joined her, his body shuddering against hers and his breath leaving him with a groan.

Breathless, heart pounding, he lay on top of her, all the time careful of his weight, his strength, knowing that he could so easily hurt her in the throes of passion.

"I should turn you," he murmured against her damp skin.

"What?" She pushed against his shoulders.

"I have to be so careful with you, so aware of how easy it is to hurt you, but if I turned you, well, two birds with one stone." Her narrowed eyes told him she wasn't following, and the way she was pushing him off her told him she wasn't thrilled with his idea so far.

He ran a hand through his hair, blowing out a breath.

"God, it makes perfect sense. I don't know why I didn't think of it before. I'll turn you. Then you'll no longer be weak. And you can spend more time with Skye without worrying about her going for your jugular. And, as an added bonus, I won't have to hold back when we have sex." He raised his eyes to look at her, expecting a smile of agreement. Instead, she was glowering at him, furious. He frowned in confusion.

"I'm weak?" Her voice was level but vibrating with emotion, "You won't have to hold back when we have sex? So what, I'm some pathetic, useless lay, am I? All this time, having sex with an 'inferior' human when you'd rather be banging a vampire?"

He looked stunned. "Georgia, that's not what I meant," he pleaded as she slid off the table and darted out of reach. He had to admit she was surprisingly fast for a human. There it was again. *Human.*

"Oh, I think that's exactly what you meant, Zak. You said it yourself. You've been holding back with me, so you don't hurt me. Because I'm weak, vulnerable, a puny human." She angrily pulled on her jeans and jerked her tank top over her head, not bothering with her underwear, leaving the flimsy garments on the floor.

"I..." He had nothing. She was right; it was how he felt, only he hadn't realized it himself until the words fell out of his mouth. Each time he'd thrust into her, he was careful, knowing he could easily lose control and injure her. He never fully let himself go.

Angry tears sparkled in her eyes, and he cursed. He didn't mean that he didn't desire her, that she couldn't bring him to his knees with her touch, her kiss. That the moments they'd had together so far hadn't been... breathtaking. He wouldn't change any of it. But if she were stronger, faster, he wouldn't have to worry quite so much. Having rough sex was an added bonus, but the sex wasn't what this was about. It was about the fact that Marius was coming, and Georgia was the weakest link. How could he possibly expect to keep her safe and alive when battling a Master Vampire when she was human. So breakable.

"I need to be able to protect you, Georgia," his own temper starting to rise, "be reasonable. I could throw you across this room with one hand and shatter your spine. That easy." He snapped his fingers to demonstrate.

"You should have led with that, vampire," her voice dripped ice, "instead of letting me believe I was enough for you. I thought you accepted what we had between us, that you accepted *me*. I trusted you, only to discover that *I'm not enough*."

He cringed at the pain in her voice. "I love you," his voice rose, "I do, and you are enough for me, I just.... hell, Georgia, you're twisting this," he accused. He must convince her this was the right course.

"You love me? You're ruining it!" she yelled.

"We end this now, Georgia. You're being foolish," he growled, his temper rising.

"Of course I am," she sneered, "never you. Because I'm the inferior one, right?" She strode out of the room.

"Georgia!" He bellowed, "Don't you walk away from me. Get back here. Now. We are not done talking."

He thought he heard her mutter, "I am," over the front door slamming. He was pulling on his pants when he heard her truck start up.

"Georgia!" he yelled, hopping on one leg as he tried to get his trousers up and run at the same time. She couldn't be leaving; she wouldn't do anything that stupid.

She did. He got to the front door in time to see the gravel fly from beneath her wheels as she reached the end of the drive and swung her truck onto the road into town.

Fuck. His hand punched clear through the wall.

GEORGIA'S TRUCK ate up the miles. It had been a long while since she'd been for a drive just for the pure joy of it. Not that she was feeling joyful right at this minute. Her jaw was clenched so tight she thought her molars might crack. She was seething. Fucking furious at the jackass. NOW the sex wasn't good enough? The heart-stopping, mind-blowing, multiple orgasm sex she'd been enjoying with him wasn't good enough? She'd thought she'd been making love with him, and all the time, he'd been holding back, not lost in the moment with her, not flying to the moon and back as the world tilted on its axis and threatened to send her hurtling off into space. He hadn't been lost in her as she had been with him. And it hurt. A lot.

She passed the turn off to her place, knowing that it would be the first place he'd look for her. She had no doubt he'd be looking but damned if he was going to find her. Not until she was good and ready.

She drove mindlessly, through the night and into dawn. Her gym bag had been on the floor of the passenger side, and she'd stopped to rifle through it, see what she had at her disposal. In the bottom had been a coin purse with a few coins and a credit card she'd kept there for emergencies. Well, didn't this qualify as one? Having your heart stomped on by the one you loved counted as an emergency in her book.

Knowing Aston would probably track any electronic transactions she made, she stopped at the ATM in Redmeadows and pulled out as much as the machine would allow in one hit. Then she'd hit the road, heading up the coast. Finally, at mid-morning, she pulled over, fatigue pulling at her, making her eyelids droop. It wasn't safe to keep driving. She'd fall asleep at the wheel and prove Zak right. Fragile little human. Stretching out across the front seats, she slept, paying no heed to the tears that silently leaked from her eyes.

"She's gone." Zak slumped in his chair, his hands loose on the conference table. The same table only hours ago he'd taken her on, reveled in her. Then ruined her. He'd mishandled it all. He shouldn't have brought up sex at all. He'd made her feel she was lacking, that she was unable to satisfy him, but that wasn't true. She was his everything. He didn't mind holding back with her if it meant he could feel her shatter in his arms, that she could draw from him his own mind-melting orgasms. With her, it was perfect. Right. But his careless words had pushed her away. He'd searched for her, transporting to her farm, the pub, the shop, other pubs. He couldn't find her.

"You know Georgia," Skye consoled him with a pat on the shoulder, "She's hot-headed. That girl always had a temper. She'll cool off."

"It's not safe for her out there alone," he muttered, dropping his head onto his hands on the table.

"You see, saying shit like that is what pissed her

off in the first place. Georgia's been fighting her own battles for a long time, Zak. Then you come along, love her, teach her, rescue her, worship her and then whip it all out from under her by complaining that she's human."

"But it's true. Humans are frail."

"So she was right? That you want to turn her so you can have rough sex without fracturing her pelvis?"

"No!"

"Well, geez, Zak, that's sure what it sounded like." Of course, the whole household heard their fight.

"I told her she'd be able to spend more time with you, that you wouldn't be distracted by her blood if she wasn't human. And that she'd be stronger, more able to fight a vampire."

"Those points were kinda secondary to the sex part."

"I know." He groaned again. "Shouldn't have mentioned sex. Especially after we'd just finished..."

"What you're asking of her isn't any small thing," Skye spoke softly, her words for him alone. "I had no choice, no say in it, so my situation is different. Don't get me wrong, I'm glad you turned me, otherwise I wouldn't be here at all. But adapting to being a different species is huge, Zak. I can't go outside in the sun anymore. I won't be able to run the shop anymore. Instead of eating my favorite foods, I'm drinking blood. Life, as I knew it, is simply not the same. Suddenly springing that on Georgia? C'mon, how did you expect her to react?"

"What you say is true," he gritted, hating himself. He'd handled this all wrong. Now he just hoped she'd give him the chance to make it right.

FORTY-EIGHT HOURS. It had taken forty-eight hours for her anger to burn itself out. The first twelve were a blur as she'd driven as hard and as far away as she could get. Then she'd found a pub and, as was her usual style, drank herself into oblivion. Then slept it off. And twelve hours to drive back, calmer, but no happier.

Turning into his driveway, nothing had changed except for everything. She'd barely turned off the ignition when the driver's side door was wrenched open, and he was there, cupping her face oh so gently in shaking hands and kissing her, softly, over, and over.

"I'm sorry. So, so, sorry," he whispered against

her lips. She melted. Stupid vampire. Not able to form the words that she'd forgiven him; instead, she opened her mouth, scoring her tongue on one of his fangs. Their blood kiss heated her, sending her pulse racing and a delicious heat to settle low.

"I take it I'm forgiven." He needed the words, she realized. She wasn't sure she could give them to him. Pulling away, she looked into his dark eyes.

"For now, vampire." The best she could do. Clasping hands, he led her inside, where she was greeted with hugs and slaps on the back. She'd been missed. It hit her that she'd missed these guys as well, that she thought of them as family. And here was her actual family, her sister Skye, now a vampire. Maybe Zak's idea hadn't been so off.

"We need to talk," she told him, leading the way upstairs to his bedroom. Closing the door, she paced while he sat on the edge of the bed. The silence stretched between them.

"I don't want to rehash what's already been said," she started, stopping to look at him before pacing again. He nodded, remaining silent, letting her lead. "You know you hurt me, right? But I'm pretty sure you didn't mean to, that perhaps you didn't choose your words wisely." He was nodding, so she continued, "And I guess I'm known for my knee-jerk reactions and a short fuse." He was still nodding until she frowned at him. He stopped.

"I've spoken with Skye." His head jerked in surprise, "Yeah, she didn't tell you that, did she?"

"She didn't," he growled.

"Because I asked her not to. I rang while I was away. We talked about her new life, what it's like for her, her regrets, if any. My quandary is that I have a choice. That I can agree to this, or not. That there are consequences either way. If I allow you to turn me, my whole world will change. If I don't? Well, that's all in the air, isn't it, but you seem convinced my life expectancy is pretty short."

"We all change. It doesn't mean we lose who we are."

"True. I've seen for myself, with Skye. So... I've decided..." she paused, eyeing him. He was so still he could have been a statue. A handsome, sexy vampire. "I'll do it. I'm not ready to die, and Marius will not get away with what he did to me. He'll not expect you to turn me since you've kept me human all this time. And the fucking sex better be friggin' amazing, or I might stake you myself."

He laughed, swooping her up and spinning her around in his arms.

"You are amazing. You are strong, feisty,

unbelievably sexy, and I love you so much I think my heart just might explode." His mouth came down on hers, crushing her against him.

"When?" he growled against her lips.

"No time like the present." She shivered in his embrace, suddenly nervous.

"You don't want to talk to Skye first?"

"She knows. We decided together when I phoned. And don't get mad at her for not telling you. I made her swear, and she is my sister first, your protégé second."

"I may disagree with that."

"Not if you're smart."

Again he laughed. "We'll need a bit of preparation first. Get some fresh blood in for you; you'll need it when the thirst arrives."

"Don't you have blood here?"

"Enough to take care of the men and Skye, but newborns have a raging thirst. We'll need more. Don't fret. I'll send Kyan and Heath out to source more while we get started."

He kissed her again, hard, then disappeared. She crossed to sit on the edge of the bed to wait. Within a minute, he was back. Grinning.

"Don't look so triumphant." She grimaced.

"Sorry. The men are thrilled that you will be joining the ranks."

"The ranks? I get to be a warrior?"

"Only if you want to."

"Well, there's a career choice I'd never considered." She played with her fingers nervously in her lap. A large hand came down over hers, and she stilled.

"Don't be afraid."

"I'm still human. I'm afraid," she admitted.

"Skye would have told you what she went through? The transition?" Georgia nodded. "The only difference is I need to drain you first. Then give you my blood. Then you'll sleep. When you awake, the transition will be upon you, and it'll hurt. We may have to lock you in a cell to keep you from harming yourself or others while the bloodlust is upon you. I won't leave you alone; I'll be there with you every step of the way. I promise."

She nodded. Right. Locked in a cell. She shuddered. She didn't want to be locked in a cell. Ever again. She stood, started pacing again, her breathing jagged, her pulse strummed loud enough he could hear it from across the room.

He moved to her, reaching out to catch the single tear that rolled down her cheek. As soon as he touched her, Georgia's whole body began to tremble.

"Just do it." Her voice was no more than a whisper, and she didn't look at him. His hand caressed her cheek, then he pulled her into his arms, hearing her heart rate triple as his head dipped to her throat.

"Zak..."

"Shh," he whispered, resting a finger against her lips as he held her in an unbreakable grip. "Don't fear. We'll get through this together. I love you."

Then he buried his fangs in her throat, right into the pulsating vein that thrummed in unison with her heartbeat. Georgia moaned, her hands grasping his shoulders. Zak drew his teeth out, allowing a stream of hot, sweet blood to fill his mouth.

He swallowed the richness of her blood, his fingers moving into the thickness of her hair. Then he slid his fangs into her jugular again, deeper this time, sinking them to the hilt. Georgia shuddered against him, the blood loss making her sway on her feet. His arms tightened around her, holding her body and her throat closer to him as he bit her a third time, the three sets of twin punctures sending Georgia's blood shooting into his mouth as fast as he could swallow it.

His entire body began to feel heated, heavier, and humming with the energy he absorbed with every swallow. Feeling Georgia's blood pour into him, merging them together more thoroughly than sex ever could, caused a heady exhilaration to flare through him. Georgia would never be closer to anyone than she was to him at this moment, her life force draining from her and flowing into him, tying them together with a bond that could never be undone.

When Georgia hung limply in his arms, her heartbeat all but silent except for a few stubborn, intermittent flutters, Zak pulled away from her throat at last. Her eyes were closed, her mouth slightly open, her breathing stopped.

Pulling a pocketknife from his back pocket, he dug it into his neck, tearing the flesh, then held Georgia's mouth to the wound. He could feel her body react to the blood. Zak kept her pressed to his neck until the wound closed, and then he tore it open again with the pocketknife. This time, he didn't need to assist Georgia in swallowing his blood; her throat worked even as her heart fell silent for the last time.

Zak cradled her to him, reveling in the small pain as she fastened her teeth onto his neck and sucked, stronger and stronger. He maneuvered them to the bed, sat with his back against the headboard with Georgia straddling him, knees by his hips, chest to chest, mouth never leaving his throat. He celebrated the pain of her bite as she chewed at him with little finesse because, in each desperate swallow, Georgia absorbed life from him just as he had from her.

Eventually, he pulled away, restraining her when she would have fought to return to his throat. Her eyes sprung open, blood red, and two fangs curved out from Georgia's previously flat upper teeth. A last shudder tore through her, then her eyes rolled back, and she slumped against him, her humanity gone, her new vampire body unconscious but soon to rise.

TWENTY-FIVE

Georgia was trapped in a roaring inferno. She could feel the agony of the flames as they ravaged her body and peeled away her skin. And then relief, washing over her burned, broken body, easing the torment that seared her from the inside out.

She could taste something incredible. Something so rich and succulent, it made the inferno fade into obscurity. She needed more of that, whatever it was.

Then that amazing nectar was gone, and the inferno claimed her once more, flames dancing across her skin, burning her eyes, peeling the skin from bones, and leaving her nothing but a burnt, charred mess. She whimpered.

"Georgia."

Her name. She focused on her name, dragging herself toward whoever had spoken it. Eyes fluttered open, squinting against the flames that threatened to burn them. Suddenly, she saw Zak's face right in front of her, his dark eyes glittering like diamonds, his skin so smooth and perfect. Zak. He had killed her... and brought her back.

A loud boom sounded behind her. Georgia jumped, sure that the house was falling down around them, the sound had been so loud, and it vibrated all around her. Zak pressed her down, preventing her from running. A jolt went through her as soon as his hands touched her skin. It felt like his entire body was electrified, currents shooting through her.

"It's just the door swinging closed, Georgia. You are in no danger." Georgia looked at him, focused solely on him and his sparkling, mesmerizing eyes. His hand cupped her jaw, and again his touch seared her, shooting sparks through her body to pool low in her abdomen.

"Relax. You've not adjusted to your new senses yet. Everything is louder, clearer, sharper. You'll get used to it, but to begin with, it could feel a little overwhelming."

Your new senses. A little overwhelming. Amidst the sizzling voltage that seared into her from Zak's hands, the continual booming around her, a strange mix of scents, and the flashes of light that burnt her eyes, Georgia's mind was seized with one single, unbelievable thought: she was no longer human.

"I'm...you..." Blindly, her hand reached out to feel her neck. Nothing but smooth skin. No wounds. No pulse.

I'm a vampire.

Zak said nothing, his hand still cupping her face. His thumb caressed her skin, and a thousand volts followed the movement, sparking through her, making her gasp and arch, whether toward him for more or away for relief, she couldn't say. Her eyes left his, gaze locking on his neck. He had no wound, but she could see dried blood on his shirt. She strained closer to sniff, catching the scent of ambrosia, stretching to latch her teeth into the fabric and suck.

He chuckled, easing her away, the fabric tearing as she refused. "Easy," he soothed, something in his hand more appealing than the dried blood on his shirt. He tilted her head, and sweet syrup poured down her throat, easing the burn, dampening the flames that had been licking all around her. All too soon, the ecstasy of that nectar was gone, and she groaned.

"What's happening to me?" she whispered.

"Bloodlust. It'll be over soon; we just have to ride it out."

She looked up at him, leaning over her. He looked different. Sharper. She could make out the different shades of black in his hair, for the first time noticing that his eyes did, in fact, have faint lines of red in them, hidden in his irises that she'd never seen before.

"You're beautiful."

"So are you. You take my breath away." He lowered his mouth to hers, allowing their lips to lightly touch. Again, her nerve endings sizzled with the contact.

"Why are you electric?"

"I'm not." He chuckled again, "You're super sensitive right now. It'll settle."

Unbidden, a surge of lust powered through her. "I want you!" she gasped, arching her hips and pushing against him. Then the flames returned. *No, no, no.* She didn't want the fire. She wanted Zak, wanted his hot body on her, in her, around her. Her temper flared along with the heat, and she bellowed her frustration. Something clasped her wrists and pinned them next to her head, then a heavy weight across her, stopping her struggles. All the while, the fire burned, the flames licked, and she thought she was dying. She fought and struggled, no way was death going to claim her now, but she was soon empty, defenseless against it as she sunk into oblivion.

SLOWLY GEORGIA OPENED HER EYES. The flames had stopped; she was no longer on fire. Moving only her eyes, she scanned the room. Where was she? A cell. Yes, Zak had warned her, hadn't he? That it was safer for her in a cell while the bloodlust was upon her. Across from her, she could see a bed in total disarray, legs bent, the whole frame twisted, the mattress sideways, dark stains on it. The walls had deep gouges and purple smears. The floor was littered with empty blood bags. Did she do this carnage? Surely not?

"Don't panic. I've got you. It's okay." Zak's voice rumbled in her ear. She realized they were on the floor. He was propped up against the wall in the corner with her between his drawn-up legs, her back pressed up against his chest and a strong arm across her stomach, keeping her pinned in place. Caged by his body.

"Zak?"

"You're safe," he assured her. She nodded, indicating she'd heard him. He didn't loosen his grip, but he wasn't hurting her.

"So. Bloodlust, eh?" she indicated the mess in front of them.

"Indeed. Do you remember?" She shook her head. No. Vague memories of fire and burning and soothing, cooling ambrosia in her mouth.

"You weren't happy being in the cell. Whenever you were lucid enough to know where you were, you lost it."

"Lost it?"

"Totally. Fought tooth and nail to get out. Took three of us to subdue you the first time. Dainton is probably going to be walking with a limp for a week."

"I *hurt* him?" she asked incredulously.

"Where it matters most," Zak assured her. "It must have slipped his mind that you're not beneath fighting dirty if you want out bad enough."

"How did I hurt him?" She asked suspiciously, "*Where* did I hurt him?"

"You bit him. In the groin." He felt her stiffen in his arms, quickly adding, "Through his fatigues."

"Oh gross. Oh yuk. I bit his...?"

"You did." She could hear the grin in his voice.

"You'd better not think this is funny," she warned, feeling his chest rumble behind her. "I didn't, you know, sever it or cause long-lasting damage, did I?" She cringed at the thought.

"He's fine," Zak assured her, loosening his hold slightly. "Though it's doubtful he'll live it down among the guys."

"Tell me I bit and let go. Tell me I didn't latch on and?"

"No way I'm ever going to let you drink from anyone but me!" Zak growled, "No matter where your fangs land. Rest assured, I pried you off him."

Georgia relaxed against him. His touch was no longer an electric current but a pleasant buzz up and down her spine. Delicious.

"And all this?" she waved her hand around the room, at the gouges in the brickwork. "Did I do this?"

"You were quite the hellcat. I didn't think being in a cell would torture you so; I was wrong, and for that, I am sorry. I should have anticipated your panic about being restrained in this way."

"It's done. But can we go now? Am I okay to leave?"

"Yes. Bloodlust will still hit you, and it'll come on quickly, but you're through the transition."

"Good. 'Cos, I could really use a shower." She was covered in dried blood, her clothing torn and filthy.

Georgia caught sight of herself in the large mirror above the sink when Zak transported them upstairs to his bathroom. The bright overhead lights hurt her eyes, so he'd immediately turned them off, lighting the candles that littered the countertop. In the flicker of candlelight, she studied her reflection. Zak leaned against the door jam, watching.

She looked the same, yet different. Her skin wasn't as tanned as before, but she wasn't totally pale. Her freckles were gone, and her skin appeared poreless. While her hair was dirty and the ends matted, it looked thicker, more lustrous, deeper shades of chocolate layered throughout, the pink streaks brighter, more vibrant. Her eyes were no longer green but glowing red. Zak had warned her about this, that in the early days, they'd be red, but the green would return as she became acclimatized to her new body.

Her hand fluttered up to her throat, not a mark

or blemish in sight. She pulled her collar aside and gasped when the fabric tore, as flimsy as a cobweb.

"Touch everything as if it were made of eggshells," Zak advised, "You'll break lots of things before you get used to your strength."

She nodded in acknowledgment, brushing her hands down her front but not gentle enough. Her shirt was now a torn rag at her feet. No matter, it was ruined with all the blood anyway. Her eyes went back to her reflection, searching for differences in her body. Were her breasts perter? Fuller? She edged a bra strap aside and was left gaping when that too was left hanging in her hand, torn. She heard Zak swallow and turned her head to look at him. His eyes were on her breasts, his tongue sweeping along his lower lip.

She looked back at the mirror, at her once dusky-colored nipples that were now a deep, almost glistening red. She admitted they really were quite stunning, turning her shoulders and examining them from different angles. What else had changed? Wriggling out of her jeans, she studied her naked body. The most significant change was her skin tone, her tan lines gone, and her skin had an all-over luminous glow, topped with berry red nipples.

"You like?" she queried, not looking at Zak but still running enraptured eyes over her reflection.

"Very much," he growled, pushing away from the doorframe and stalking toward her, his eyes glowing. She turned toward him, watching him as intently as he was her.

"Do you like?" he arched a brow, his eyes dropping to her chest. She ran her hands up over her rib cage and cupped herself.

"Oh yes!" she breathed. "I wasn't expecting these changes." She grinned in delight.

He moved closer still, crowding her. She backed up, allowing him to steer her backward into the shower stall. With a flick, the water streamed from the showerhead, temperature pre-set to a wondrous warmth. The needles of water bounced off her skin, a sensation she'd never felt before, kinda like acupuncture on steroids. Then Zak was in with her, clothes and all. Grabbing the loofa hanging over the tap handle, he squirted soap on it and began washing her, spinning her around. He started at the nape of her neck before working his way down to her feet, turning her again and working his way back up.

"Touch me," she begged when he softly ran the loofah between her legs.

"Not yet," he growled, continuing his upward journey. Finally, he reached her neck, dragging the sudsy loofah across her collarbone before letting it drop to the tiled floor. With trembling hands, he cupped her face and brought her mouth to his. Her mouth was hot, wet, delectable. He explored her with his tongue, scraping across her fangs until she could taste his blood. She groaned, rubbing up against him, needing more, her blood burning through her veins for more, more of him, his taste, his scent. She mimicked his movements, thrusting her own tongue into his mouth and scraping her tongue across his fangs, her blood flooding his mouth.

With a roar, he grasped her against him, pushing her upper body against the cool tiles, lifting her off her feet. Instinctively she wrapped her legs around his waist.

"Don't let me hurt you," she breathed, tearing her mouth from the kiss.

"You can't," he assured her, capturing her mouth again and thrusting his tongue inside, mimicking his hips thrusting against her.

"You're overdressed."

"So I am." He shucked out of his clothes in record

time, leaving them in a wet pile on the shower floor. "Now, where were we?" He lifted her again; when her legs went around him, her core hovered tantalizingly close to his cock. He chuckled when he felt her wriggle her hips, trying to initiate contact.

"Nuh-uh. I have some making up to do."

"What?" She frowned, thrusting against him in frustration. Tilting her hips, she ground herself against his stomach, the friction delicious, the scent of her arousal surrounding them.

"You're killing me here," he growled, mouth dropping to her neck where he sucked, pulling her vein close to the surface and laving it with his tongue. One hand wrapped around her waist, keeping her pinned to the wall; the other glided across her wet flesh, cupping the weight of her breast. His thumb flicked across her nipple, and she whimpered, writhing against him. His head lowered, capturing the bud in his mouth and laving her nipple with his tongue.

"Oh, God... Zak!" She pushed herself further into his mouth. "More. Please." Her body wriggled and writhed, wet and slippery against him, every touch burning. Every nerve ending was heightened, every touch super sensitive, pushing her closer to the edge. Christ, she was about to come, and he hadn't touched her *there* yet.

He lowered her legs to the floor, keeping an arm around her waist to steady her. His mouth moved to her other breast, biting and teasing, her red nipples becoming tighter, darker. She was mewling, small noises in the back of her throat while her fingers dug into his scalp, fisting his hair. He knelt before her, pulling her thigh over his shoulder as his lips trailed lower, across her ribcage and abdomen, pausing at her navel to dip and play before going lower still.

"Zaaaakkkkk," she begged, needing his touch, the anticipation killing her. Then he was there, his hot mouth closing over her, his tongue pushing between her folds, lapping at her in long strokes. Her legs wobbled, and he pushed her harder against the tile, keeping her upright while his tongue pushed deeper, harder, faster. A finger joined the action, pushing into her, then withdrawing, over and over. A second finger, then a third, pushing her wider, feeling her walls clench around him. He pumped her, and she writhed against him, pressing herself against him. He kept her hovering on the edge, withdrawing his fingers, slowing his tongue.

"No, no, no," she wept.

He curled a finger up inside her, searching for and finding the small smooth ridge, stroking over it while he laved her clit with his tongue again and again. She shattered, her climax screaming against the walls as she fell apart around him, drenching his hand, her walls tight against his finger as his tongue continued its relentless pulsing against her. Finally, he withdrew, allowing her to slide down the wall, so she was sitting before him, legs spread, eyes closed, a dazed expression on her face.

Opening her eyes, she gazed at him, her irises redder than ever.

"Oh. My. Fucking. God."

"Good?" he grinned, pride in his voice.

"Incredible," she agreed, slowly coming to her senses. A different hunger hit her, driving every other thought out of her head.

"Feed." His voice sounded so far away. Then her face was pressed into his neck. Without thought, her fangs sank into his flesh, and she drank, bliss pouring down her throat, heavier than water, sweeter than syrup. This time it was he who groaned against her, pressing his erection into her stomach and rocking. Minutes passed until, sated, she pulled her fangs from his flesh, running her tongue over the wounds to seal them. He pulled away from her, erection straining but looking at her with a strange expression on his face.

"What?" she asked defensively, "what did I do wrong?"

"Nothing... you... you stopped drinking. On your own, I didn't have to pull you off. Then you sealed the wounds. I hadn't even taught you that yet."

"Guess I'm just rocking this vampire business then." She grinned cockily. She eyed his erection. "Let's take this to the bedroom. There's something I want to do." He didn't have to be asked twice. Rising to his feet, he flicked off the shower, pulled her to her feet, and wrapped her in a towel.

"I'm going to finish you off in a way you've only dreamed of," she purred. He almost came listening to her sultry voice and the wicked things she promised. Who knew Georgia would turn into such a sexual siren now she was a vampire?

She threw the towel over her shoulder and walked loosely across to the bed, hips swaying.

"Come," she purred, eyes dark with passion, "stand before me, Zak." Her eyes lovingly took in the muscles tapering from his broad chest down to his narrow hips, his erection jutting proudly. He moved to where she sat on the edge of the bed.

"Hold yourself," she commanded. One brow arched, but he did as she requested, taking his shaft into his hand.

"Bring it to my lips," she whispered. He groaned, easing himself to her mouth where she licked the tip. Leaning forward, she ran her tongue over the head. He groaned. She grinned. His skin was so smooth, so sensitive. She gazed up at him, running her tongue along the slit.

"Delicious," her voice deepening into a husky growl. "Don't blow too soon, Zak," she warned, "I'm just getting started."

She lifted her hand and fit her fingers along his shaft, feeling him pulsate in her palm. She stroked him, his breath whistling between gritted teeth when her fingers brushed his balls. A drop of moisture beaded, and she ran her tongue around it.

"Suck me," he begged. She leisurely swirled her tongue over the tip again, then drew him deeper, licking as she sucked. She pumped her fist on his shaft as her mouth followed in time, her free hand cradling and stroking his balls.

"I'm about..." His voice was ragged, his hips rocking. She upped the pace, greedy for his release, wanting to feel it, to taste it.

"...to come..." His body froze, and with a roar, he

climaxed. With a final groan, he pulled away, and she collapsed back on the bed, a grin on her lips. How primal.

Zak flopped next to her, breathing hard. She turned her head to find him watching her.

"You are *the* most beautiful, sexiest woman I have ever laid eyes on," he murmured, his hand lazily tracing patterns across her stomach. He propped himself on one elbow, head resting on his palm as he continued to allow his fingers to drift across her skin. He'd loved her body when she was human, but now her skin glowed with luminosity, pale but hypersensitive.

"Zak," she purred back-arching, seeking more of his touch. He was hard, again. Grabbing her, he dragged her further up the bed, settling himself between her thighs. His hand dipped to the core of her. She was so hot and wet, ready for him.

With one swift thrust, he entered her, withdrew, plunged into her again, twisting his hips to make Georgia feel things she didn't know she could.

She began to orgasm almost immediately. She could feel herself clenching his shaft again and again while he shuddered and sweated above her, already on the verge himself.

"Oh God," she cried, her orgasm continuing on,

his cock sliding inside her, never easing the pressure, the pace. He was merciless, kept plunging, plunging, driving her higher.

"Harder!" she demanded.

"You want it hard?" With a growl, he flipped her over, pulling her to her knees. Knowing what he wanted, she rose up on her elbows, ass in the air. With his hands clamped on her hips, he pounded into her. Her forehead lowered to the mattress, exposing the nape of her neck. He moved his body over hers, hips still thrusting, and sank his teeth into that exposed flesh at the back of her neck. She screamed, her climax clenching him so hard it was as if she'd had him in her fist. He released her neck and straightened, thrusting harder. She reached up and braced herself against the headboard, her upright position adding more friction. His hands swept up the front of her body, grabbing her breasts and pinching her nipples. She pushed back against him, harder, harder.

So close, he was so close. Needed to take her with him. While one hand continued to pinch and squeeze at her breasts, his other delved between her legs, rubbing against her clit, pressing, releasing, massaging, tickling. He could feel her muscles tensing, feel the tension building, and he pounded harder. Almost there.

Another scream. She shattered, arching, hips pushing back into him and her head falling forward. Yes, yes, yes. His balls drew up tight. He sank his fangs into her neck, and his climax hit him, roaring through his blood, hips surging forward uncontrollably, pistoning between her thighs, emptying into her over and over.

He pulled her into his arms as they collapsed onto the bed. He pressed a kiss to her damp temple and whispered soothing words as she struggled to calm her thundering heart. She laid a limp hand against her chest, feeling the beat.

"I thought I shouldn't have a heartbeat?" she questioned.

"During the transition, you don't, then it kicks back in. Same with breathing. You don't need the oxygen anymore, but it doesn't hurt to breathe, makes us less of an anomaly when we're amongst humans."

"I hate it when you're right," she muttered.

"I don't follow." He frowned at her sudden change in subject.

"The sex. We couldn't have done it like that if I was still human, right? That was no holding back?"

"I let you have it all, baby," he agreed, stroking her. He grinned when she climbed on top of him, straddling his hips, her long hair draping around them as she leaned down to brush her lips across his mouth.

"Why do I still want more?" she whispered, her hips slowly undulating over him, the delicious friction rubbing his hard again cock against her clit.

"Remember I told you about the blood lust?" He cupped her breasts, pulling a nipple to his mouth where he laved it with his tongue.

"Urgh," was her garbled reply, tipping over the edge into a passion-filled haze.

"And I told you that sex and blood got all mixed up in this burning need?" He pushed against her, and she pressed back in return. So responsive.

"That's where you're at." His own breath caught in his throat when she fisted him, squeezing and pumping his cock. Arching into her, he nearly dislodged her from her perch on top of him.

"Nuh-uh-ah." She released him, pushing him back to the mattress. "This is my ride." Positioning herself over him and lowering, sheathing him inside her. She alternated between raising and lowering her hips, then swiveling them in a rocking motion. He'd lost count of how many times she'd climaxed;

she was relentless, wanting more, more, more. She'd slow the pace to a crawl, torturing him, then speed up, riding him fast and hard. Sitting upright and bouncing on his dick, she reached back, cupping his balls. He climaxed with a roar, bucking against her, his fingers bruising her hips where he held her on him.

CHAPTER
TWENTY-SIX

They remained in his room for two days. Two days of sex and blood, blood and sex. Georgia would never have survived as a human, but as a vampire, she was insatiable. Her blood lust was nothing compared to her lust for him. She only had to look at him, his wicked grin and sparkling eyes, and she wanted to peel off his clothes and mount him. Eventually, she knew she'd have to face the real world. Marius was still out there, and Skye was probably anxious to check on her. And Zak needed to check in on his warriors.

Stretching, she slid off the bed. Shower and dress. She could *feel* him watching her, knew if she turned and met his gaze, she'd be back in his bed, and it'd be another twenty-four hours before they surfaced.

"Cut it out," she growled, striding across the room and grabbing the bathroom door handle, only to have it come off in her hand. *What the?*

"Eggshells, Georgia," Zak reminded her. Right, right. She was super strong now. He'd told her to touch everything as if it were made of eggshells, except him. She could touch and squeeze him as hard as she liked. Which she did. Often.

Giving what she hoped was a gentle push, the bathroom door fell off its hinges. Ok, not eggshell level yet. Casting distressed eyes to him, he nodded in encouragement. Almost too scared to touch the light switch, she gently gave the lightest touch with her forefinger. The light came on without sparking or fizzing. Buoyed by her success, she moved over to the shower, reaching in to flick the tap on. *She muttered careful, careful, careful*, brows drawn together in concentration. It felt like she'd barely made contact when the water began streaming from the showerhead. Pleased she hadn't ripped the plumbing from the wall, she stepped beneath the spray. Ahhh, the water over her sensitive skin was almost sexual, like a million fingers caressing her.

Cut it out, she told herself, quickly cleaning her

body and washing her hair. She stepped out, not trusting herself to linger under the seductive spray. Back in the bedroom, Zak had tossed some clothes on the bed for her, and again, she carefully picked them up and dressed. Success, no tears. Zak was dressed and waiting for her, handsome in black fatigues. Her hair was still wrapped in a towel, and he moved behind her to massage her scalp and dry the still dripping ends. He ordered her to sit on the bed while he knelt behind her and gently combed the tangles out of her hair, the long waist-length strands curling around his fingers as he worked.

"I need you to stop," Georgia growled, blood heating and pooling, the familiar desire surging through her at breakneck speeds.

"What if I don't want to?" He swept her hair back from her neck and kissed her skin.

Suddenly she was on top of him, pushing him down while straddling his hips. He laughed.

"We'll never leave this room again if you don't stop leading me on. I can't resist you."

As much as he loved her passion and insatiable thirst for him, Zak could see the distress in her eyes. He grabbed her by the shoulders and transported them to the door, setting her away from him.

"It's okay, love," he promised, "we'll keep you to

bagged blood when outside of our room. And if it looks like you're about to tear my clothes off and have your way with me, I'll transport us back here." He knew she was worried she'd disgrace herself by shagging him in front of everyone.

Georgia nodded. Hand on the doorknob, she gently turned, this time opening the door without damaging it. She threw him a triumphant grin over her shoulder as he followed her out.

She halted at the top of the stairs. Looking down, the warriors and Skye had gathered. She could feel them watching her, all eyes intent. Rattled, she took a step back, bumping into Zak, who steadied her with a hand on her hip.

"They're not going to hurt you," he whispered in her ear, then eyed his warriors, his gaze demanding they back down. "They're a little unbelieving that you could have gotten your blood lust under control so quickly. They think you'll fly off the handle any second."

She looked at him. "I won't, will I?"

"Doubtful. You have amazing control." His innuendo was clear, and she elbowed him in the ribs.

They descended the stairs, side by side, hand in hand. At the bottom, Skye pushed forward and hugged her. The warriors relaxed and gathered around Zak, updating him on what had been happening over the last few days—not much—and their plan of attack on Marius. They drifted toward the conference room, and Georgia could actually feel his presence pulling away from her, like a shadow of herself. She stood with Skye and watched the others leave while examining the bond between her and Zak, stretching, stretching, stretching. But it didn't break. It just stretched and flexed between them, never breaking but always there. So this is what it meant to be blood bonded, she mused.

"You look amazing." Skye smiled at her, standing back and running her eyes over her sister.

"You know, I can't remember the last time I saw you with your hair down." She touched the silken strands that curled over Georgia's shoulders and dropped almost to her waist.

"Necessity at the moment," Georgia admitted, "I keep breaking the hair ties, and Zak is crap at braiding it."

"I'm so jealous," Skye admitted.

"Of my hair?" Georgia was stunned.

"No, silly," Skye giggled, "that you've beaten your blood lust in mere days. It took me weeks."

"What about the other?" Georgia lowered her voice.

"The other?"

"Sex. Physical lust. I'm having *a lot* of trouble with controlling that."

"Oh! Well, um, it hasn't been too bad for me. An odd twinge. Plus, Zak has strictly forbidden them to touch me, so even if I wanted to, none of them would go against Zak."

"I don't understand," Georgia muttered.

"Maybe it's because you and Zak were already, you know, doing it?" Skye offered. Georgia's mind drifted, remembering her and Zak *doing it* and her pulse quickened, her eyes darkened.

"Georgia!" Skye shook her. "Focus. Let me show you where the blood's kept." Skye grabbed her hand and led her to the kitchen. The fridge was stacked with blood bags.

"I like mine warm," Skye told her. Grabbing a coffee cup and a blood bag, she pierced the bag, draining the contents into the mug and placing it in the microwave. "Try it."

Georgia took the mug and sipped. Not too bad. Nothing like the sweetness of Zak's blood, but bearable.

"Have you tried fresh blood?" Georgia asked her sister.

"Yeah. It's divine. Dainton showed me, just in case I was somewhere, and the thirst hit me, and I couldn't get to our supply. He said it was important I learn to drink from the vein without harming the humans. And how to trance them into forgetting."

The humans. Only a few short days ago, Georgia was human. And not long before that, so was Skye. And here they were, standing in Zak's kitchen drinking blood out of coffee cups. She never saw that coming.

While they chatted, Georgia examined the newly renovated kitchen. It had a country-industrial vibe, white cupboards, tiles, and stainless-steel appliances. The kitchen table seated eight comfortably and had a French provincial feel. Small pots with herbs sat upon the windowsill, adding to the charm.

"We need to decide what to do about the shop."

"God, the shop! The fire seemed soooo long ago. Do we know how the clean-up and repairs are going?"

"I haven't been able to get down there and check."

"Okay, okay. Let me think. Obviously, we can't

run it as a nine-to-five store anymore. Neither of us would be able to show up during the day. What about after hours? Do you know the zoning laws?"

"I did look into it, but to be honest, I think we should just sell," Skye admitted.

"Really? But you love that place," Georgia protested.

"I know, but all that has changed. And I've had longer to get my head around this being a vampire thing, and having the shop isn't viable. I can't go back to living above the shop, and I don't want to. I like it here. I've got my own room; the guys are great. This is my life now."

Georgia absorbed Skye's words, stunned. An invisible weight lifted from her shoulders. Skye was happy and content in her new vampire life. And Georgia knew she would be too.

"And the farm?" Skye asked.

"Not sure. Guess I'll have to sell as well. I still have a mortgage, and if we're not bringing in income from the shop, I won't be able to afford it. I'm probably already behind in payments, with everything that's gone on for the last few weeks."

Georgia stood and stretched. "I want to go back and get some more of my stuff. Are you all moved in here, or do you still have clothes there?"

"I've only got what the guys shoved into a bag for me," Skye admitted. That was all Georgia had as well. That decided, she stuck her head into the conference room.

"Sorry to interrupt, fellas. Zak, Skye, and I are dropping into the farm to pick up some gear."

"No."

"Too bad. We're going." She shut the door, but he'd teleported next to her within a second.

"It's not safe."

"Zak, nothing has happened since I've been back, and it's been days. A couple of hours at the farm getting some of my stuff won't hurt. You can't dump us here with a handful of clothes and expect us to call it 'home.' Us girls need our things, and I, for one, need more hair ties!"

"I don't like it."

"You don't have to, but you know I don't cope well with being smothered. And perhaps just a little bit of distance will help me get this *ache* under control." Now that he was next to her, touching her, her body was on fire again, want and need thrumming through her.

His eyes darkened and dropped to her mouth. He rubbed his thumb along her full lower lip, and her tongue darted out to taste him.

"Go," he growled, his own control slipping. "But take this." He pressed a cell phone into her hand. "Two hours. You'd both better be back safe and sound." He slipped back into the conference room, the door clicking closed in the silence that followed.

"Wow!" Skye was impressed. "You've got him wrapped around your little finger."

"I'm not sure who's got who," Georgia admitted, struggling to come down from the high just being close to him brought.

HER FRONT DOOR was sealed with 'Police. Do not cross' ribbon. She could see the residue from fingerprinting dust, and she suddenly remembered.

"Rhys!" Shit. Rhys. Her best friend. Her best friend, who she hadn't given a thought to in how long? Three weeks? Four? Okay, she had a pretty good reason, being held captive by Marius for three of those weeks, but he'd never crossed her mind since her return. Damn it.

"Shit," she muttered, feeling bad. Ignoring the tape, she pushed inside. Everything was exactly how they left it the night Skye was taken. Furniture overturned, bloodstains on walls and floors. Skye's bedroom window was broken, the fly screen torn. The girls righted the furniture then quickly packed what they could. While Skye was loading the truck, Georgia pulled out the phone Zak had given her and dialed a familiar number.

"Yeah?" A familiar gruff growl.

"Rhys? It's Georgia." She heard feet hit the floor, could almost see him sitting up straight.

"Georgia! Fuck. Where are you? Are you okay? Shit, I've been looking for you for a month!" he rushed.

"I'm home. I'm fine," she assured him. "I'm sorry I worried you."

"Stay put!" He hung up.

"Was that wise?" Skye asked from the doorway. Georgia shrugged. Maybe not, but if Rhys found out she was back, and Zak wouldn't let him see her? It wasn't fair. Rhys loved and cared about both of them, and he deserved answers. And the truth.

He must've broken every speed limit in the city, tires spinning as he skidded to a halt in the driveway. Rushing inside, he came to an abrupt halt when he saw them, standing side by side, red eyes glowing.

"Fucking. Hell," he ground out, running a trembling hand through his thick hair, the strands sticking up on end. "You've gone vamp," he spat, anger pulsing across the room. Georgia felt it like a physical thing, pushing at her. She growled, fangs popping from her gums.

"Hey, hey, hey," Skye soothed, one hand against Georgia's chest, the other held toward Rhys, palm out. "Let's just calm down. Rhys, c'mon, not like you to jump to conclusions," she chided him. His breath left him in a whoosh, and he collapsed into an armchair, rubbing a weary hand across his eyes.

"Thought you two were fucking dead," he muttered, his voice torn, the pain evident.

"We're sorry," Skye murmured softly, easing her hand away from Georgia's chest but keeping a close eye on her sister. She'd only been risen a few days; it wasn't wise to put Rhys's juicy arteries in the same room with her.

Georgia remained frozen in place while Skye filled Rhys in on what went down and how they both now appeared before him as vampires. She didn't know if vampires drank werewolf blood, but Rhys smelt pretty good to her right now. She backed up, not leaving the room but putting herself as far away as she could but still keeping him in sight. Over the burn of her hunger was raw emotion. She'd missed him, but with her change, their relationship had changed. Irrevocably. They wouldn't be hanging out anymore, and she mourned the loss.

Rhys eyed her, his gaze full of pain and disappointment.

"Stop looking at me like that," she growled, his pain feeding her own. All her emotions were heightened, his pain scraping raw like salt in a wound. He looked away, then his head snapped to the left, sniffing the air.

"Company." He jumped to his feet. "Vamps." Back to the wall, he inched toward the window and peered out. "Not your guys."

"Fucking typical," Georgia swore, "now Marius decides to make his move."

"Do you think he knew we left the homestead?" Skye murmured.

"Possibly. Makes sense. We need to get back to Zak." Georgia's heart was beating too fast, panic starting to blanket her vision in red. Memories of the pain she'd suffered at the hands of Marius had her trembling and shaking, losing control. They had to get out. Get away. Now. The sounds, sights, scents, it was all too much. She felt like she was going to explode out of her skin.

SOMETHING WET COATED her face and mouth. Licking it, she craved more.

"Easy now, pet," a voice soothed from far away. More wetness filled her mouth and slid down her throat, soothing the burn. Her shaking stopped, and her eyes blinked open. Everything was filtered through a haze of red. "What?" her voice was hoarse.

"Georgia." Zak's voice. She was with Zak. She was safe. The haze started to clear, senses returning. She was on the floor in Zak's kitchen, empty blood bags strewn around her.

"How'd I get here?"

"It was amazing!" Skye declared, kneeling by her side, and helping her sit up. Warriors stood around them, and Rhys sat uneasily at the kitchen table, uncomfortable in a vampire's lair. How did they get out of the farm with Marius approaching?

"You teleported! Not just yourself, you swooped us up into a giant bear hug and teleported us here," Skye told her, voice laced with excitement.

"Bullshit." Georgia pulled herself to her feet, wiping her forearm across her face, blood smearing.

"It's true," Zak confirmed. "The three of you suddenly appeared right here. Of course, the effort totally drained you, sending you into immediate blood lust." That explained the carnage on the kitchen floor. She looked over at Rhys, who was pale beneath his tan. "Did I hurt you?"

"No."

Thank God. She'd never forgive herself if she hurt him. She looked back to Zak.

"Blood bags? Not you?"

"If it was Marius at your farm, then he is on his way here. I need to keep my strength." He brushed a thumb across her cheekbone. Without conscious thought, she was in his arms, pressed into him from knee to chest, arms wrapped around his neck and mouth planted on his. She propelled them across the room, crashing him back against the wall, plaster falling around them. His hand cupped the back of her head, and he tilted his head, changing the angle of their kiss, spinning them, so it was she who was pushed up against the wall. Capturing her wrists, he pinned them above her head, and she groaned into his mouth. More. His hand came up to cup her breast when the sound of a male clearing his throat penetrated the fog. They both froze, then Zak slowly and gently disengaged. He waited for her to calm, to catch her breath, not touching her but shielding her body from view while she struggled to get her lust under control.

"I'm good." She straightened her clothes and

squared her shoulders. There was no time to feel embarrassed; the house began to vibrate.

"Do you feel that?" Aston muttered. They did. Everyone scattered to the front of the house in time to see the front door explode, ripped off the hinges by an invisible force. The door crashed onto the floor with a thud that seemed to reverberate throughout the entire house.

Marius strode in, power rolling from him in great waves. Behind him came Erik, Veronica, and a dozen others. Silence filled the large foyer, the Warriors still and silent, weapons drawn.

Marius's eyes landed on her, cold and assessing.

"Lost your humanity so soon?" he sneered.

"Don't speak to me, parasite," she hissed, the red haze dancing at the edges of her vision.

"No matter. Now that you've turned, you're more likely to survive me bedding you. Raping you as a human would have been a delight, but now in your new body? I can't wait."

Zak let an enraged roar, and while everything happened at once, at the same time, it was as if time had frozen. Around her, the sounds of battle reached her ears. Flesh tearing heads rolling, blood spraying. She felt isolated from it. In the middle of it, yet not.

"Bitch!" She was knocked back into awareness

by a body on her back, clawing at her face. Veronica. Grabbing the woman by the arm, she swung hard, flipping her over her shoulder and onto the floor in front of her. The tiles cracked at the impact. Georgia leaped on her, and they rolled, Veronica managing to plunge a blade into Georgia's side. Georgia tried to reach her dagger, tucked inside her boot, but couldn't get to it. She'd have to do this the hard way. Pulling her arm back, she plunged her hand into Veronica's abdomen, pushing up under her ribcage and squeezing her heart in her fist.

Veronica gurgled, blood sputtering from her mouth as she tried to slide away on her back. Georgia straddled her, arm still buried in her chest, still squeezing. Veronica's eyes were shocked.

"You know, I wonder if your heart really is black?" she asked conversationally. She pulled the organ free with a tug, holding it up in her clenched fist, gore and blood running down her arm.

"Well look at that. Red like the rest of us." She glanced down at the other woman, eyes frozen in death.

As soon as Marius threatened Georgia, Zak's control snapped. Simply vanished. Pure rage washed through him as he launched himself at the other vampire, plowing into him and sending them both flying across the room, their air-bound flight coming to a sudden halt when they hit the wall, dust and rubble falling around them.

Zak was quickly on his feet, launching another attack, determined to rip Marius's head off and end this threat once and for all. Georgia's dagger could kill him for good, but so could removing his head. And Marius knew it. Deftly he avoided Zak's attack, managing to stay out of reach.

Zak could feel his magic stirring, pushing at his control. He couldn't let it out, not here; he'd end up killing them all. He knew the moment his eyes glowed green—Marius's breath hitched in his throat, and for a second, he froze, stunned by the change. He could probably feel Zak's power rolling over him as well.

"What are you?"

"More than you." His voice was deeper, the magic seeping through him taking over, changing him, making him stronger, more powerful. "More than you'll ever be. You think because you've awoken that you can do what you want? Take what you want?"

"You were careless with her," Marius sneered, "leading her straight into danger. You don't deserve her."

"Maybe not, but she is mine nonetheless. *Mine.*" The pain of losing Georgia, of knowing the torture Marius forced on her, was too much. Emotion rolled through him, gathering momentum he was powerless to control. With a roar, a wave of power shot from his hand; he would make this vampire pay with his life. Nothing less would do.

Marius tried to dodge, but it was futile. He flew across the room again, smashing into another wall, the powerful wave not easing up as it forced him through wall after wall until he was at the far end of the house. Shakily he rose to his feet, watching as Zak stalked through the holes in the walls towards him, eyes glowing green and promising death.

STILL STRADDLING Veronica's lifeless body, Georgia looked around her. The battle raged, Zak and Marius trading blows across the room from her. Suddenly a hand tangled in her hair and jerked her backward off

Veronica's body. Georgia wriggled and tried to twist away, but her hair was wrapped around and around someone's wrist, dragging her back across the blood-splattered floor until they were out of sight. Then she was thrown across the floor. Sliding to a stop, she pushed her hair out of her eyes to face her attacker. Erik. Should've known.

"You and I have some unfinished business." He stalked toward her, eyes gleaming, fangs extended. Georgia sprang into a crouch, ready for him.

"You were promised to me," Erik told her conversationally as they circled around each other, waiting for the other to pounce. "Once Marius had finished with you, he was giving you to me. I'm here to take what's mine."

"I'm not yours, and I'm not Marius's either, dickwad."

Erik lunged, but she was ready for him, ducking and rolling out of the way. He growled in frustration but kept up the pursuit.

"You're going to taste so fucking good."

"You're never going to know."

Rather than wait for his next attack, Georgia pounced, springing at him only to duck low at the last minute, cannonballing into his lower body, knocking him off his feet. They skidded across the floor, knocking furniture over with their momentum. She managed to latch onto his back, forearm across his throat, and legs wrapped in a punishing grip around his middle. She pulled tighter and tighter, trying to break his neck, but she had the wrong angle. Strangling him wouldn't achieve anything; he didn't need air to breathe. He struggled to his knees with her on his back, then slammed himself backward, crushing her against a wall. It was enough to loosen her grip, and he flipped, pinning her to the wall. He grinned, baring fangs as he started to lower his mouth to her neck. He wasn't expecting the head butt that had him seeing stars. Nor the following sharp, burning pain of her dagger piercing his chest and sinking into his heart.

"I said no," Georgia gritted, twisting the dagger and shredding his heart, "and when a girl says no, she damn well means it, asshole." His eyes met hers, surprise and confusion flashing across his face as he died, sliding sideways to the floor.

She was pushing him away from her, struggling to get out from beneath his deadweight where he'd pinned her against the wall when she saw Marius blast through the wall, backward. Only he didn't stop but flew across the room and through the next wall. Zak followed a second later, stalking across the room and stepping through the hole Marius made.

Finally getting free of Erik's body, she climbed to her feet and peered through the hole in the wall, watching with eager anticipation as Zak approached Marius, who stood dusty and shaken. Then Marius's gaze shifted to her over Zak's shoulder and his lips twisted in a sneer.

"Georgia." Her name was enough to distract Zak. He froze and began to turn. In that instant, Marius launched over him and flew toward her, so fast she couldn't react. Then he was upon her, arm tight around her throat as he used her as a shield against Zak, who was now facing them, body rigid.

"I will have her," Marius spoke, voice eerily calm.

"Never," Zak and Georgia spoke at the same time. Zak's eyes met hers, his glowing eyes mesmerizing and softening for a moment when Georgia grinned at him.

Sensing the two of them were communicating in some way, Marius bent her head back, exposing her neck. "I've missed this," he murmured, his fangs inches from piercing her skin. Rather than fight him, Georgia allowed her body to become a dead weight, sagging in his grip. He held her, staggering, and trying to keep them both upright with a grunt. She slumped lower, her smile growing, when she heard him swear.

Finally, he had no choice but to let go of her, and she let herself fall to the floor at his feet, where she palmed the dagger she'd kept hidden along her arm. With a quick twist, she swung, her blade slashing the back of his ankle. He roared in pain; his foot almost severed. She scrambled backward as he fell to his knees, his eyes black with rage.

He followed as she scooted backward, not fast enough as he clasped her ankle and yanked her back toward him. She felt his vicious fangs sink into the back of her calf and roared in outrage and pain, then brought up her free foot and kicked him in the face. He released her immediately, hands going to his face. She swung with the dagger, not even thinking about the next move, and it sank into the side of his neck.

They both froze. She kept a tight grip on the handle, not giving him the opportunity to wrench the dagger free and use it on her. The skin around the wound turned purple and dark streaks fanned out from it, like lightning dancing across his skin.

He screamed. The scream of a man in intense agony.

With whatever strength he had left, he pushed

her away from him. The dagger ripped from his neck as she slid a few feet away. Zak scooped her up, wrapping his arms protectively around her.

"Okay, baby?" he asked.

"I'm fine. Finish him."

She'd barely finished speaking before Zak was on the other man, hands gripping either side of his head, twisting until she heard an audible snap and then wrenching until a sickening tear indicated Marius's head had separated from his body. Holding Marius's head by the hair, Zak strode into the foyer, intending to bring Marius's soldiers to heel, only to discover his warriors had already dispatched them.

Georgia appeared behind him. Her eyes touched on Zak and each of the warriors, checking all were accounted for, then paused when she realized they were all looking at her.

She wiped her bloody hands on her jeans. "Errr. Look. Sorry. I know she was your friend and all, but seriously? She betrayed you all, and she was a bitch. Sorry guys, but she had it coming."

"We understand," Frank spoke up.

"You're not angry with me?"

"You were protecting yourself, love. And us. No-one here is judging you." Zak kissed the tip of her nose, then suddenly grabbed his head, groaning in pain.

"Zak?"

"Arghhhhh!" He fell to his knees, hands wrapped around his skull.

"What's happening?" Georgia cried, kneeling by his side, "Zak? Zak?" Tears streaming down her face, she watched as he toppled onto his side, convulsing. She looked around at the warriors, distraught. "What's going on? What's wrong with him?" No one had any answers.

When his convulsions stopped, they moved him to his bed. Georgia shooed them out of the room, wetting a face washer and gently cleaning the blood from his face. She cleaned him up the best she could, then took a quick shower herself, not wanting to lie on their beautiful bed and soil it with others' blood.

"Come back to me, love," she whispered, curling into his side. He lay motionless for the remainder of the night, and when daybreak hit, Georgia fell into her own slumber.

TWENTY-SEVEN

"Good morning." Mmmm, that delicious, sexy voice that she loved rumbled in her ear. She stretched, pressing her body along the length of his.

"Morning," she returned, hands already busy, running up and down his body. Then she remembered, and her eyes sprung open. She sat up, dislodging the covers that fell to her waist, exposing her naked breasts.

"You're awake!" she exclaimed, hands running over him to reassure herself he was really awake and okay.

"So are you. And looking very delectable if I may say so." He pulled her across him, mouth clamping onto one blood-red nipple. Something nagged at the back of her mind, hard to think when his mouth was doing such wicked things to her body.

"Wait. Wait." She pushed back.

"Wait? That doesn't sound like you, love," he teased, pushing the heavy curtain of her hair back over her shoulder.

"What happened? You can explain to me later why I happen to be naked when I know I was dressed when I went to sleep last night, later. Right now, I want to know what happened to you. You clutched your head, had some sort of fit, then lapsed into a catatonic state."

"I had a vision. I guess?"

"A vision? Of what?" She moved to straddle him, looking down into his face with concern.

"I don't really know! It was a jumbled, confusing mess. A dream, more like a nightmare."

"What happened?"

"I was in a different dimension. There were angels, demons, and Gods. Everyone was arguing. Lightning was surrounding this cloud-type platform they were standing on. I think they were arguing about my ring and your dagger." He ran a hand through his hair, the ends standing in every direction.

"What about them?" She ran her hands across

his chest in a soothing gesture. She knew how disconcerting it could be when someone messes with your dreams.

"It was like they were trying to decide what the ring and dagger stood for. Someone said that the ring is to be worn by the King, and the dagger shall belong to his Queen. Another argued that they're a part of an ancient protection spell to protect a witch. Someone else said when they have reunited, a child born of prophecy shall walk the Earth. A demon insisted they are bringers of good and evil, life and death. A different demon insisted they were the portal to open the gates to Hell."

"What do you think?"

"I've got no bloody idea! It was all surreal. I'm not even sure it was a vision. Maybe I had a concussion or something, I don't know, but it was downright weird, that's for sure. All they did was argue and shout over each other."

"But you're okay now? Do you feel okay? No headache?"

"Babe, I'm fine." He wriggled his hips beneath her, and she grinned; leaning down, she planted a kiss on his lips, "you feel mighty fine to me," she said into his mouth. "Now about me waking up naked?"

THE END...for now. Keep reading Georgia and Zak's story in First Witch!

Thank you for reading! If you enjoyed this book, I'd greatly appreciate your review.

You can find a complete list of my books, including series and reading order on my website at:

www.JaneHinchey.com

Join my newsletter here:

www.JaneHinchey.com/ghostly-newsflash

And finally, join my readers group on Facebook here:

www.JaneHinchey.com/LittleDevils

Thank you so much for taking a chance and reading my book . It's readers like you who make this journey worthwhile and fuel my passion for storytelling. Your support means the world to me, and I can't wait to share more exciting stories with you in the future.

xoxo
Jane

FREE BOOK OFFER

Want to get an email alert when a new book is released?

Sign up for my newsletter today, https://janehinchey.com/subscribe

and as a bonus, receive a FREE e-book of

Cupcakes & Curses!

READ MORE BY JANE

Find them all at www.JaneHinchey.com/books

The Ghost Detective Mysteries

#1 Ghost Mortem

#2 Give up the Ghost

#3 The Ghost is Clear

#4 A Ghost of a Chance

#5 Here Ghost Nothing

#6 Who Ghost There?

#7 Wild Ghost Chase

#8 Easy Come, Easy Ghost

#9 Life Ghost On

Witch Way Paranormal Cozy Mystery Series

#1 Witch Way to Magic & Mayhem

#2 Witch Way to Romance & Ruin

#3 Witch Way Down Under

#4 Witch Way to Beauty & the Beach

#5 Witch Way to Death & Destruction

#6 Witch Way to Secrets & Sorcery

The Gravestone Mysteries

#1 Fur the Hex of it

#2 Battle of the Hexes

#3 What the Hex

The Midnight Chronicles

#1 One Minute to Midnight

#2 Two Minutes Past Midnight

#3 Third Strike of Midnight

Clean Scene Inc.

#1 All in Vein

PARANORMAL ROMANCE/URBAN FANTASY

The Awakening Trilogy

Hell's Angel Trilogy

The Enforcer Series (4 books)

Standalones

Returned

Secret Fates

Destiny's Touch

Blood Cursed

Heart of Darkness

ABOUT JANE

Jane Hinchey delivers snort-worthy cozy mysteries and sizzling paranormal romances that grab readers from the get-go. With tenacious heroines, lovable sidekicks, and heroes who are more than just a pretty face, her books are an irresistible mix of humor, magic, and heart. From witches cracking cases to vampires in love, she offers an adventure where the extraordinary is the norm and love bites in the best way.

Find Jane here: www.janehinchey.com

www.ingramcontent.com/pod-product-compliance
Lightning Source LLC
Chambersburg PA
CBHW030650120726
47905CB00001B/148